A Date With Destiny

The Hallelujah Series

Lutishia Lovely

The Hallelujah Series is published by Kensington
Publishing and LDE Publishing
1350 E. Flamingo Road, Suite 102
Las Vegas, NV 89119

ISBN-10: 1535299061
ISBN013: 9-7815352990-6-0
Copyright © 2016, Lutishia Lovely.

A Summary Guide To The Hallelujah Series:

Book 1: Sex In The Sanctuary

Tai Brook and Vivian Montgomery are best friends who also happen to be pastor's wives. One has experienced fifteen years of wedded bliss. The other suspects her philandering husband is cheating again. Add to this mix church goers whose eyes are on each other when they should be on Jesus and you've got a series of problems that only God can solve.

Book 2: Love Like Hallelujah

While faithful churchgoers Hope Jones and Millicent Sims choose very different routes to the marital altar, the one thing they both do is pray. Hope patiently waits but God says nothing. Millicent is thrilled with the answer she believes she hears. But what happens when her would-be fiancé doesn't get the memo and chooses another? A happily ever after? Or hell on earth?

Book 3: A Preacher's Passion

When Passion Perkins meets Lavon Chapman she hopes that he's the answer to her "please end my celibacy" prayer. She's waited five years for Mr. Right and goes after this man in full pursuit. But while she's chasing him he's chasing someone else, and theirs is not the only situation in which three is definitely a crowd.

Book 4: Heaven Right Here

The members of Kingdom Citizens Christian Center are being fruitful and multiplying, as the Good Book commands. But when jealousies and misunderstandings lead to "baby mama drama" all hell breaks loose. Some shaken saints call on Jesus, a few call on each other and one finds out some fights in life are simply not worth having.

Book 5: Reverend Feelgood

Nathaniel "Nate" Thicke is a preaching prodigy who at the age of twenty-eight is the senior pastor of Gospel Truth Church. He's carrying on a tradition begun by his great-grandfather, in which his spiritual obligation to the flock takes the phrase "laying on of hands" to a whole new level. But what's done in darkness comes to light…for everyone.

Book 6: Heaven Forbid

When a scandal breaks out in nearby Texas, the Reverend Doctor Pastor Bishop Overseer Mister Stanley Obadiah Meshach Brook, Jr. rides to the rescue. He lays down the law with a code of ethics so strict that even Jesus might not pass muster! He calls in a spiritual son to revive this fallen congregation, but the man called in needs a little reviving himself.

Book 7: Divine Intervention

King and Tai Brook's daughter, Princess, is about to marry the man she thinks she needs until a wedding day disaster gives the man she wants a chance to try and win back her love. Her mother tries to be supportive but has problems of her own and the family matriarch, Mama Max Brook, is praying for heavenly help with the good Reverend Doctor. Because if she finds out that what she's heard is true...he's going to need it!

Book 8: The Eleventh Commandment

Without a doubt, the members of Kingdom Citizens Christian Center love God and embrace their Christianity. But when an old flame suddenly reappears and a few not-so-sacred secrets get revealed, some are having a hard time obeying the ten commandments. Then comes rule number eleven which may prove harder than all the other ten.

"For I know the plans I have for you, says the LORD. Plans to prosper you and not to harm you, plans to give you a hope and a future."
Jeremiah 29:11

The Sanctity of Sisterhood (SOS) Pledge

I'm uncommon. I'm unusual.

I am not the status quo.

Set apart, an earthly treasure

because my Father deemed it so.

Yes I am my sister's keeper

and it must be understood

that today we stand united

in the sanctity of sisterhood.

1

Outwardly, Destiny Noble-Thicke was the epitome of sophisticated calm. Inwardly, she was a bundle of nerves. It had been a year since her infamous husband, Nathaniel "Nate" Thicke, had accepted the position of senior pastor at Divine Grace Christian Center in Las Vegas, Nevada. One would think she'd be used to the scrutiny that came along with being a first lady and sitting next to him on the raised dais. She wasn't. The overt stares left her feeling like an object on display and made it way too easy to see women cut her the side eye while ogling her man. On the other hand, the position enabled her to spot who watched her. A few observations made her uncomfortable, one more than the others.

"Praise him, saints!" Reverend King Brook, guest speaker for the afternoon's celebratory service, stood as the last notes of the song he'd requested faded amid shouts and applause. "He's worthy, isn't He?"

"Yes!" Several parishioners responded.

"Amen!" Others shouted.

"Pastor,"—King looked over at Nate—"I believe there are some folk in here who know something about Jesus!"

Nate nodded and stood.

King addressed the standing-room-only crowd. "Is there anybody in here who knows the Lord?"

The din of noise grew louder.

"Somebody here knows him as a doctor. Some know Him as a lawyer. Some know Him as a friend in need and a friend indeed! Someone you can trust when all others forsake you. Oh, I guess I'm in this by myself. I must be the only one who's been lied on, mistreated, betrayed and verbally slayed."

People throughout the congregation rose to shout their responses.

"Preach!"

"Amen."

"Tell the truth!"

"At one time or another I'm sure some of you were like me. We were the ones doing the lying, the ones mistreating and the ones betraying. But one day God picked us up, turned us around, placed our feet on solid ground!"

Smiles, shouts and applause rippled through the congregation as many acknowledged coming short of God's glory and experiencing amazing grace.

"Look at your neighbor and say 'won't God do it'?"

The crowd obeyed.

"If He's ever done anything for you, big or little, large or small, I want you to stand on your feet and shout, 'God did that thang'!"

As one the congregation roared.

Another round of praise erupted, fanned by the staccato chords of the organist. The rest of the band quickly followed his lead. The choir stood and sang another chorus of the day's theme song.

God. Will. God will do it.
He'll bring you through it,
Like there's nothing to it.
Yes, God! Bless God!
Won't God do it? Yes, He will!

Destiny listened, lightly tapping a designer shoe-clad toe as she watched the choir. This understated form of worship was one of many problems some had with her exalted position. Her slender beauty, stylishly contemporary wardrobe and quiet demeanor—sometimes perceived as uppity snobbishness—were some other reasons she was disliked. Some people felt a stunning physique, two beautiful children and a handsome, successful husband were too many blessings for one woman to enjoy. A few had complained. Others had offered unsolicited advice. Some members had left the congregation. Their presence was barely missed as hordes more—mostly female—joined the church. Thirsty. Attractive. Bolder than a robed Ku Klux Klan member at an NAACP convention. Destiny handled all of this with an attitude that was cool and unperturbed. They knew her glory but not her story. Knew not the women who mentored her in being a first lady. Knew not how God had prepared her for this moment long before anyone in this town knew her name.

As the song ended and King began his sermon, Destiny turned her attention to the audience and smiled at three of those mentors seated in the front row: her grandmother, mother and the first lady whose popular Sanctity of Sisterhood Conferences helped shaped Destiny's outlook on womanhood, marriage and ministry. She schooled her features into a pleasant expression as her eyes continued down the pew to the reason her best friend, Princess, was not at the service. Princess was King Brook's daughter and about the same age as Charmaine, the second wife who graced the pew. To say the two women didn't get along was an understatement. When told that Charmaine would be there, Princess had adamantly refused to attend. Destiny understood. It had to be hard to embrace a second wife who'd climbed into the marital bed before the first wife had left it.

Much easier to show compassion for Janet Miller, the woman seated behind the new Mrs. Brook. This selfless long-time member of Divine Grace had been dealt a bad hand but praised God every Sunday in spite of it. The person dealing most of those bad cards was Ronald, the husband sitting beside her. Their eyes locked. He winked, and smiled. Destiny's skin crawled. The man's overt flirting and constant leering made her nauseous. He'd overstepped proprietary boundaries more than once and had been called out for this behavior...more than once. Not just for how he treated her, but other female members as well. Unfortunately, some women encouraged it. Like Nate, Ronald was a handsome, well-groomed chocolate drop—six foot one to Nate's six three—with enough charisma to bottle and sell. After a salacious rumor about Ronald having an affair with a pastor's wife proved to be true, Nate had issued a warning for the deacon to clean up his act. Since then Ronald had either been less promiscuous or more clandestine. The possibility of a lucrative church contract also had him on his best behavior. Still, there were moments. Like now, as he stared at her with an unreadable expression. She looked through him and focused on Janet. An apprehensive tingle snaked down her spine. Destiny got the distinct feeling that Ronald's wandering eye was not the couple's only problem.

"Are you all right, baby?"

Only as she felt Nate's hand on her arm and breath in her ear did she realize the slightest of frowns had marred her face. He was very observant, especially when it came to anything to do with her. That was only one of many things she loved about him.

"I'm fine," she whispered, catching a whiff of his musky cologne as she leaned toward him.

"No, you're not. And I suspect I know why. But Princess still could have attended."

The shift was subtle but by removing her arm and turning her body more fully toward King she effectively cut off communication with Nate. As intellectual and smart as her husband was, he could sometimes come off sounding as dumb as an ox. If he thought putting Princess and her father's new wife in the same room would go over well, even one the size of an auditorium adorned with a neon cross and filled with bibles, now was one of those times.

An hour and a half later, Nate and Destiny were whisked through a side door to join the Christian elite who'd been granted access backstage. The VIP room was appropriately appointed and held a who's who roster from both the Christian and secular worlds. Also present were members of Divine Grace's ministerial staff. The celebrated first couple was comfortable among them all, standing at the front of the room and enduring an endless parade of congratulatory well-wishers.

As the line waned, Destiny watched Ronald and Janet Miller enter the room, greet the Brooks, and head their way. She steeled her nerves and stepped closer to her husband.

Ronald came smiling with hand outstretched.

"Excellent service, Reverend. That was some of the finest preaching I've heard in a while."

Nate shook Ronald's hand. "King Brook is one of the best."

"That's what I told him." An usher tapped Nate to pull him aside. Nate addressed the group. "Excuse me for a moment."

As Nate stepped away, Ronald stepped closer and reached for Destiny's hand. "Good afternoon, First Lady."

"Deacon Miller." Her tone was even and barely warm.

Not wanting to make a scene she offered a tight smile as he raised her hand to his lips and gently kissed it.

"You're looking more beautiful than this perfect May weather."

"Not as beautiful as Mrs. Miller," Destiny said to Janet, while all but yanking free the hand that Ronald still held and covertly stroked with his thumb.

She wanted to slap him. But people were watching.

Janet raised her hand to hide a crooked smile, glancing at Ronald before responding. "Why thank you, Lady Destiny."

"I was admiring your suit earlier. I love that shade of blue on you. The necklace pulls everything together perfectly. What type of stones are they?" She took a step toward Janet on the pretense of examining her jewelry. What she really wanted was a closer look at the bruise she thought she'd seen from the dais.

"I don't know," Janet replied with a nervous chuckle. "It's just costume jewelry."

"Well, it's gorgeous." Destiny looked over the shorter woman's shoulder and smiled as two of her favorite women approached and Nate returned. "Janet, meet my mother." She gently turned Janet around, effectively shutting Ronald out of the circle. "This is my mom, Simone Simmons, and her mother, Katherine Noble. Mom, Kat, this is Janet Miller. Her husband, Ron," Destiny nodded toward Ronald who was now chatting with Nate, "is our head deacon and director of finance."

The ladies exchanged introductions. "It's easy to see where Destiny gets her beauty," Janet said sincerely. She looked at Katherine. "And you're her grandmother?"

"Not hardly," Katherine drawled, attitude dripping amid the sarcasm.

"Oh, I'm sorry." Janet looked at Destiny. "I thought you said—"

"I did." Destiny's eyes shined with humor. "The G-word isn't one that Kat embraces. Janet is one of our most faithful members," she said to Katherine, "and a part of the team of ladies who help me in the ministry. She's been a member of this congregation for a very long time."

"Ladies!" Ronald invaded their circle. "The good reverend here is being remiss so I must take it upon myself to meet the sunshine lighting up the room." He turned to Simone and offered his hand. "My name is Ronald Miller. Would you by any chance be related to our stunning first lady?"

"I would, indeed," Simone responded with a smile. "I'm her mother, Simone Simmons, and this is my mother, Katherine Noble."

"Ah, yes. Your husband is the former governor of Louisiana."

"That is correct."

Ronald turned to Katherine but addressed Simone. "And you say this is your sister?"

"My mother."

"Can't be."

"It's true."

She shook his hand. He held it and topped it with his other hand. "It is my pleasure to meet you."

"Likewise," Katherine replied, responding to the flirtation with enough sugary sweetness to bring on diabetes and unlike her granddaughter, not pulling her hand away.

Ronald's smile widened. "How long are you ladies in town?"

"I'm not sure," Kat purred. "We—"

"Are leaving," Destiny interrupted. She turned to Nate. "Babe?"

"Sure, we can do that. I was just about to send a text to have the car brought around."

As if on cue, Nate's valet approached. "Reverend, are you and the first lady ready to go? Your dinner reservation is in less than two hours."

"See, that's why you're my man. Anticipating my needs before I can call you." He reached for Destiny's hand and motioned to the others. "Let's go."

The first couple and their entourage made proper goodbyes and left the room. Destiny smiled and waved, giving what she hoped were appropriate responses to questions she barely heard. Showing restraint in the face of Ronald's callous behavior was exhausting. His flirting with her grandmother was callous and rude. Concern for Janet made her insides roil, along with trying to determine how much of what had transpired this afternoon should be shared with her hot-tempered husband. It all felt like a bad storm coming, one in which you gathered your family, stayed at home and waited for it to pass. That wasn't possible, so she kept up a pleasant façade. They were getting ready to host an elaborate dinner. But Destiny had lost her appetite.

2

Because of the anniversary program that afternoon there was no night service at Divine Grace. Instead, the Thickes had reserved the private room of an upscale restaurant and invited several of the out-of-town pastors and wives who'd attended the anniversary to be their guests. The group included some of their favorite people: King Brook (and for decorum, his wife Charmaine), Derrick and Vivian Montgomery, Stan and Passion Lee, Lavon and Carla Chapman, Cy and Hope Taylor and the Thicke's second-couple-in-command, Ben and Savannah Harvey. These were not only pastors but good friends who spent entirely too little time together, a fact that made the conversation lively, the laughter loud and opinions blatantly honest. Nate gave off a jovial appearance, while privately worrying about a wife who hadn't been herself since the anniversary program ended. When asked about what was going on, Destiny said she'd tell him after dinner. For Nate the end of the evening couldn't come soon enough.

"I can't believe it's been a year already." Derrick Montgomery took the last bite of a perfectly cooked filet. "Are you glad to be back in ministry?"

"For the most part," Nate replied. "But I miss the

heck out of the Turks and island life."

"Did you own your home there?" Derrick's wife Vivian asked Destiny. She nodded. "Did you sell it?"

Destiny forced a smile and took a sip of tea. "I don't know that we'll ever sell that house. We made wonderful memories there and great friends. plus it is where our daughter was born. So far the ministry has kept us too busy to take a vacation but we're hoping to go early next year."

"I don't blame you for keeping it." Cy Taylor was a member of Derrick's church. When Nate and Destiny lived in Turks and Caicos, he and his wife, Hope, had visited them. "It's a beautiful home in a prime location. A good investment to pass on to your kids."

Stan Lee, who pastored a church in Los Angeles, nodded his head. "I don't blame you either. Some of the drama these saints are creating right now makes me wish I had a home on an island."

"What's going on?" Nate asked.

Stan gave him a look. "Never mind, brother. You don't even want to know."

Carla Chapman, a former preacher's wife and recently retired national talk show host, was all too familiar with church drama. Some of it her own. "I want to know something." She turned to Nate who was sitting beside her. "It looks as though overall you have a good, supportive ministerial team. But what's up with those Miller men?"

Nate felt Destiny stiffen as she made an almost inaudible sound of disgust. He was sure the others hadn't noticed but considering her earlier comment and ongoing subdued mood, his radar was up.

"They're longtime members who led the campaign against my hiring. Under the previous minister, Roy was the assistant, and thought he should have been promoted to senior pastor. He'd served in the position for ten years so I can't say I blame him. His brother, Ronald, is a successful contractor—arrogant, conceited. He had the last pastor in his back pocket but knows that I had to be convinced to allow him to keep the position of head deacon and finance committee chair. Both have an eye for ladies other than their wives, though Ronald has been known to do more than look."

Carla sighed dramatically. "What a surprise. Another man who can't keep his pecker private."

This elicited various humored responses.

"Unfortunately," Nate continued, "I was once one of those men. So I've tried not to be overly judgmental. There are still problems. But for the most part it appears the brothers have gotten on board and are now supportive of our vision. Given the circumstances that's saying a lot."

"You still might want to keep a close eye on the situation," Derrick suggested. "Especially the preacher." As pastor of Kingdom Citizens Christian Center, one of the largest and most popular churches in Los Angeles, his counsel was sound. "I've dealt with my share of jealousy and envy—"

"And has the knife scars on his back to prove it," his wife, Vivian, interjected.

"You're wise to keep him close and on staff. But I wouldn't make him a confidante."

"That would never happen," Nate replied. He pushed back from the table and placed his hands behind his head. "He and his brother are close. I wouldn't trust Ron as far as I could throw him."

He looked at Destiny. She averted her eyes, though too late for him not to notice the discomfort they revealed. Again, Nate silently vowed that the night wouldn't pass without finding out why.

"He's the tall, commanding looking brother who presided over the offering?" Nate looked at King, who'd asked the question, and nodded. "And you don't trust him?"

"No, but I don't think he'll steal money. He has his own. Besides, we have several safeguards in place, including a rather elaborate camera security system."

"What happened to trusting in God and putting our faith in Him?" Stan spoke with a measured cadence that made him sound like he was preaching even now.

"God said in all our getting to get understanding," Nate replied. "So since I understand that the devil is busy, and that the mind is willing but the flesh is weak, I got some extra security to make sure that the tithes don't end up in the home of Pookie-n-nem."

The laughter this elicited was intentional, as was the way his wife's body relaxed when he placed a hand on her thigh.

"How many members were there when you started?" Passion asked.

Nate looked at Destiny. "What would you say, darling, around two-hundred, two-fifty?"

Destiny nodded. "Around that many, maybe three-hundred."

"How many were in the audience today?"

"Over a thousand, easy," Ben answered.

"Brother, you're going to need a new building soon," King said.

"Already on it, brother," Nate said. "In the planning stages as we speak."

"Are you looking for a place," Cy asked, "or constructing a new edifice?"

"We haven't decided. Finding the right building would be optimum but we're not opposed to constructing from the ground up."

"Trust me, you don't want to go that route," King said. "Took us almost two years to finish what was supposed to happen in nine months, and let's not even talk about how the budget got busted."

"Whether we build from the ground up or find a place to renovate, we'll want the project completed in six to nine months. We're already two weeks into May. My goal is to be in the new church by Christmas, or February at the latest."

"And Ron is a contractor?" King asked.

Nate nodded. "And before you ask, yes, he believes that his company getting the job is a done deal."

Derrick looked over. "Is it?"

Nate looked at Destiny before answering. "Not even close." He paused, and took a drink of tea.

"We'll have to do something, and soon. Some of the ministers are pressing me to go to two services. I don't want to do that."

"Members will work you to death if you let them," Derrick warned. "Be sure to save time for your family and private time for God."

"Oh, I'm going to do that for sure," Nate said, reaching for Destiny's hand and bringing it to his lips to kiss it. "Nothing interferes with my spending quality time with the Father, my kids, or my weekly date with Destiny."

"All right, brother," Carla purred, giving a flirty

look to her husband, Lavon. "The best kind of heat is a home fire burning."

Simone nodded thoughtfully and said, "A date with destiny. I like that."

The appetizers arrived and the conversation shifted from Divine Grace to the superb quality of the food and the happenings in other ministries. Destiny was grateful the topic of conversation had changed, and that her side discussion with Vivian about the upcoming Sanctity of Sisterhood conference took her mind totally off more troubling matters. The time would come soon enough when she'd have to confirm what she believed was happening in the Miller household…and decide what she planned to do about it.

3

Later that night, with guests gone and children tucked in, Nate and Destiny were finally alone in their master suite. Nate lay naked, on top of the covers, his mind like a video replaying the day.

Destiny came out of the en suite bathroom running fingers through still damp hair. She wore a short nightie that hit mid-thigh, and nothing else.

Nate was immediately at attention, in more ways than one. "Feel better, baby?" His eyes drank in her loveliness as she climbed on the bed. He scooted over and pulled back the covers so they both could crawl beneath them.

"A little bit," she responded, once she'd snuggled against him. She ran her fingers down his toned abs and farther down to his hardening manhood. "I know something that would help me feel even better, though."

In a rare move, Nate halted foreplay and gently pulled her stroking hand away from his jewels. "I'm definitely going to take care of that my love." He kissed her temple. "But not until we talk about what happened today that put you in such a mood."

"Let's talk about that tomorrow." Destiny threw a creamy caramel leg over his and rubbed her bare breasts against his chest. "I need you," she whispered, sucking his earlobe into her mouth and grinding against him.

"Baby," Nate groaned, forcing himself to stay in control. He loved nothing better than sexing his wife and in a little bit he'd give her all she could handle and a little more. But right now he would not be distracted. "Tell me what happened today."

Destiny sighed, and sat up against the headboard.

Nate sat up, too. "Part of it was Princess not being here I'm sure but after the service your mood changed again. Then there was the way you reacted when Carla mentioned the Millers. You tensed up like somebody shot you. Is Ron up to his old tricks again?"

A pause and then, "Yes."

Nate turned to look her in the eye. His voice turned low, deadly. "Talk to me."

"Baby, promise me you won't get upset."

"I promise nothing, Destiny. What did he do?"

"His old tricks, like you said—flirting and being inappropriate, looking at me like I'm a meal and he's man dying of hunger. You saw him flirt with Kat."

"And I saw her flirt right back."

"Which didn't surprise either of us."

"Nope."

"His leering at women is disgusting. And with his wife standing right beside him!"

Nate pulled Destiny into his arms. "Darling, the way you look, trust me, every man breathing wants a taste. But most have enough discipline to not telegraph the message."

"For a long while he was respectful, polite. I thought he'd changed."

"No, he was just busy screwing the pastor's wife."

"A-hole."

"I'm going to give him a final warning to leave you alone."

Destiny sat up and away from Nate. "Please don't."

"Why not? It's continuing to make you uncomfortable and that's not okay."

"I can handle Ronald. What I can't handle is what I think he's doing to Janet."

"Baby, you can't do anything about that either. If a woman wants to stay while her man is cheating—"

"I'm not talking about that. I'm talking about the bruise I saw her on face today. I think Ron is being abusive."

"You saw a mark on her? You're sure?"

"I can't say absolutely positively but I'm ninety-five percent sure that what I saw under her carefully applied makeup was a bruise. And there was something in her eyes when she looked me. Sadness and...fear."

"Somebody came to me with that allegation right after we first got here."

"Seriously?" Nate nodded. "What did you do?"

"I asked him point blank if he was beating his wife. He flat out denied it. His brother backed him up. So unless Janet speaks up or there's more solid proof...nothing can be done about it. That's if it's really happening."

Destiny took a deep breath. "I know what I saw. Maybe I'll ask her about it."

"I don't know, babe. If it's something that Janet wants to discuss she'll come to you."

"I've heard that many women in abusive situations are too scared to share what's happening with anyone. By the time she gets the courage it might be too late."

"Still, that's business between a man and his wife unless they, or she, requests your counsel."

"Even though in my spirit I know something's wrong?"

"So you're saying that God is telling you that Ron is physically abusing his wife?"

"In a way."

"I don't feel good about it, darling. In the middle of someone else's marriage is never a good place to be."

"You're right. But I'm Janet's first lady and her sister in Christ. And like the Sanctity of Sisterhood creed states, 'I am my sister's keeper.' So I'll try not to get in the middle but from my position on the sidelines? I'll definitely be watching."

Nate lay on the pillow and pulled Destiny down with him. He untied the ribbon that kept her bodice together. "While you're watching that," he said softly, placing kisses on her breasts between each word, "I'll be handling this."

He pulled off the nightie and tossed it away, flicked her nipple with his tongue, made lazy circles around her areola. Destiny gasped. She turned toward him and ran her hands up and down his muscled arms, back and chest. Nate's hands were busy too, stroking her stomach down to her heat. He parted her folds and placed a finger inside. Soon his tongue went on a similar journey. Destiny thrashed, tossed this way and that, cried out in ecstasy.

It was only the beginning. As he placed a pillow beneath her and eased eight thick inches of feel good into her welcoming warmth, Destiny released anxiety and experienced true joy for the first time all day. For the next hour and into her dreams, Reverend Nathaniel "Nate" Thicke was the only man on her mind.

4

The next afternoon the Noble women took advantage of the perfect, seventy-five degree spring weather with an impromptu shopping spree. Destiny's closets were already overflowing, but so what. Nothing could get her mind off the Millers and church drama like a good dose of retail therapy. Here, it was guaranteed that the only swiping would be with a credit card.

"Just one more store!"

Destiny turned to her mother and huffed. "Seriously? Don't they have stores in New Orleans?" Simone laughed. "My feet hurt!"

Simone looked at her daughter's strappy sandals. "You knew we were going shopping. Nobody told you to wear stilettos."

"I always wear heels. Just not on a marathon." She looked at her grandmother. "How about you, Kat? More shopping or a bite to eat? We have an hour before our spa appointment."

"I'm down for whatever."

"Ha!" Destiny reached for Katherine's hand and gave it a squeeze. "Of course you are! Always. I'm so glad you came, Kat." She entwined her hand with her mother's and grandmother's hands. "I didn't realize how much I've missed you guys."

"You saw us what, a little over a year ago?"

"Exactly a year." Simone answered the question that Katherine had meant for Destiny.

"Because Daniel had just turned five. And he's grown so much since then! He's going to be tall, like his father."

"Sade's going to be tall, too," Destiny said.

"And a stunner, just like her..."

"Grandmother!" Simone and Destiny said together. They burst out laughing.

Destiny saw Katherine's exasperated look. "I'm sorry, and I know you don't like the title. But 'just like her Kat' sounds indecent."

At this, even Katherine had to smile. "Speaking of indecent, why did you change the spelling of that child's name? Now instead of calling her Sadie, everyone is going to pronounce it like the singer from London."

"It was always Sade, pronounced Sadie, and always spelled that way. The hospital spelled it incorrectly when she was born and I was going through too much to deal with changing the birth certificate. Once back in the states, I took the time to correct it."

"I like that spelling," Simone said. "It's a modern twist on an old name."

"Thank you, Mom." Destiny gave Kat a look that read "so there."

The ladies entered Crystals, one of Destiny's favorite places to buy off the rack, and headed straight for Roberto Cavalli's line. Destiny immediately saw a dress perfect for Simone, a sleek black dress made of stretch jersey with long sleeves and a crystal-covered clasp accenting the waist. Kat reached for an Asian-inspired silk and chiffon caftan, its blue and black material embellished with patches of patterned fabric, and ladylike ruffles at the neck and sleeves.

A sales clerk came over to assist in the shopping and soon had Kat and Simone in the dressing room trying on clothes.

Destiny chose several more items and passed them along to her mother and Katherine. Back on the floor, a jacket caught her eye. She removed it from the hanger and walked to a three-way mirror to try it on. She'd just finished her last step-touch-turn when she looked in the mirror and glimpsed a familiar face besides her own. She whirled around, looked across the room, left and right, but saw no one. She shrugged, sure that she was mistaken anyway. The face she thought she'd seen reminded Destiny of someone she'd left in the past on purpose.

She continued shopping, glancing up every now and then to check the aisle for the phantom face before forcing herself to focus on what was really important...chic combinations of stretch jerseys and textured knits. No one needed another little black dress less than she did but that didn't stop her from taking a sleeveless mock neck off the rack and putting it up against her toned, five-foot seven frame. The flounced hem brushed her thighs, made her feel fun and feminine. Of course, she had to buy it. This was therapy after all. She tried it on and liked it so much that she decided to get the same style in a summery tangerine. She'd just found the orange one in her size and walked to the mirror when she felt a shift in the atmosphere. A second later she heard her name.

"Destiny Noble."

Destiny's hands stilled at the sound of the voice—gratingly familiar. She pulled her features into a mask of calm, then looked at the woman's image now visible in the mirror.

Slowly she turned and gave the woman a quick once-over. What she'd thought was a figment of her imagination was actually standing before her, in living color. A rush of hurtful memories increased her heartbeat. Melody Anderson, the girl whom she'd befriended at a Christian private high school and shared college confidences, then ended the friendship after being betrayed. The catalyst that thrust her husband into a national scandal and caused a rift in her marriage. None of the inner turmoil from these memories showed on her face. If Kat had taught her anything it was never to let anyone see you sweat.

They stared in silence. Melody took a step closer. "Do you still hate me?"

Destiny held Melody's gaze, noted the shadow within her perfectly made-up eyes. "I don't hate you, Melody. You're not worth the energy of that emotion. I forgave you years ago."

Melody's only response to this well-placed jab was a raised brow. "The last I heard, you and Nate lived in Turks and Caicos." No response. "Are you here on vacation?"

"Are you?"

Anyone else may have shivered at the chill in her query but Melody laughed. "You're looking the part of a well-cared for first lady—clothes right, body snatched, hair, nails and make-up on point. But beneath all of that you're the same girl I met that day in the mall. I had to pry answers out of you then, too. Took me a while to find out why. So what…another juicy secret got your mouth on mute?"

Destiny juggled mixed emotions and sarcastic comebacks behind a face that continued to show no angst. "I'm quiet because you're still talking. That mouth of yours was always a problem. You're right. Not much has changed."

"Actually, for me, everything has changed. I'm not that same broke down girl you knew in Louisiana and Dallas after that. This is my town. Trust me—I handle my business."

"You live here?"

"Ha! Do you?" Melody mimicked Destiny. "Yes, I live here."

Destiny's eyes narrowed. "Since when?"

"Since a black knight in a shiny Bentley swooped my ass up and placed me in his palace. Almost three years now. What's with that look? Ah, wait a minute. Don't tell me you live here, too."

"Actually yes, I do."

"Well, I'll be damned. Y'all left paradise and moved to sin city? Or is it just you? Did you and Nate get div—"

"Don't get your hopes up, Melody. Nate and I are still very much married and pastoring a church nearby. That's what brought us here."

"Nate's back in the pulpit?"

The taunt was a tempting morsel but Destiny didn't bite. "Are you sure you didn't know that already?"

"You think I'm here because of your husband? I haven't thought about y'all in years, much less cared about where you were living. Our living in the same town is pure coincidence."

Destiny calmly crossed her arms. "Is it the same

coincidence that moved you from Baton Rouge to Dallas so you could be close to Nate?"

"Girl, nobody wants that whore but you."

Destiny barely contained the quip "it takes one to know one." Although true it would have sounded childish. Both of them were way past grown. She struggled to hold on to calm when all she wanted was a smack down.

"You wanted him once," she said instead. "And you helped him hold that title."

Just when it looked like this verbal sparring match might go fifteen rounds Melody shrugged and backed down. "Like I said, I've been here for years. I've got a man. A good one, too. Plus, me and church don't go together. Haven't for a long time. Never did, as a matter of fact." Melody shook her head. "It's a small world."

Destiny took in Melody's perfectly put together look. The designer clothes. Diamond jewelry. What looked like an enhanced face and set of breasts courtesy of a surgeon's skillful hand.

"Too small sometimes. But it looks like life, your man, or both, are treating you well."

"I have no complaints."

"Are you married?"

"Ha! Yes, to money. My man and I have an understanding that works for both of us."

"He's what brought you to Vegas?"

"No, I met him after I arrived. Dancing brought me here. Becoming part-owner of the gentleman's club where I held star billing is why I stayed."

"I can see you being a star of the pole."

"It's Sin City," Melody replied, not at all bothered by Destiny's dig. "Sin is very profitable. And yes, I'm a master of poles. Just ask your husband."

Destiny took a step toward Melody just as Katherine exited the dressing room and walked toward them.

With a glaring last look Destiny shifted her attention to Katherine. "Did any of it work out for you?"

"It all did."

"Good. Let's ring it up." Destiny started toward the checkout, leaving Melody in the aisle. When it came to her messy past nemesis there was no need for goodbye.

"Hey, Destiny."

Destiny paused, turned.

"What's the name of your church?"

"Why, since you and church don't go together?"

Melody chuckled. "You're being awfully defensive for someone whose marriage is supposedly going so well."

"It's Divine Grace," Destiny quickly countered. "That indescribable measure of love from God that helped me not hate you."

Without waiting for a response, Destiny met Katherine at the counter.

"Who was that?" Katherine asked.

"A former friend and one of Nate's biggest mistakes."

The interrogation Destiny was sure would follow was interrupted by her vibrating phone. She quickly pulled it from her bag. "Hey, Princess. I was going to call you later."

Simone came out of the dressing room and joined them at the counter.

"Hold on a second." Destiny reached into her purse and pulled out a charge card. "Use this, Kat, for both of your purchases."

"Honey, we don't need to—"

"Shh! My treat, remember?" She walked a short distance away from Kat and Simone, thanking God for her best friend's interruption as she unmuted the call. "Girl, your timing is perfect."

"Well, you're late." Destiny didn't miss the slight irritation that accompanied Princess's words. "I thought I would have heard from you last night."

"I'm sorry. It was a full day, a long night, and my family is still here."

"Then I guess I'll let you off the hook," Princess said with a laugh. "Family can be problematic. I have one, too."

"Actually, this has been a great family visit. I hadn't seen everybody in a while and it was their first time in our new home. They leave tomorrow, but my day will be full doing everything I couldn't handle this weekend. So I'll call you Wednesday. But don't worry. What I have to tell you will be worth the wait."

"What did that heifah do, embarrass my dad?"

Destiny knew Princess was talking about Charmaine, the wicked stepmother only slightly older than her best friend.

"Charmaine? She was fine. If I didn't know the history, I'd actually like her. It's the heifah, as you say, I just ran into that's real news."

"Who?"

"Melody."

"Why does that name sound familiar?"

"Listen, I can't talk now. But like I said, I'll call you on Wednesday. Text me a time when you have at least an hour to talk. I have a million things to discuss. This conversation will take at least that long."

5

On Wednesday afternoon, Destiny gave her nanny a break and entertained her two rambunctious children. Daniel Nathaniel, named after his paternal grandfather and Nate, was almost six. Sade was three. And twenty-four year old Destiny, whom some had envisioned becoming a superstar model or celebrity actor who'd marry late and never have kids, had been doing exactly what she'd wanted to do for the past two hours—forget about problems and enjoy her family.

Her cell phone message indicator beeped. In the second she turned her head to grab the phone, havoc erupted.

"Ow! Mommy, Sade hit me. Again!"

Destiny looked sternly at the little girl with Nate's face. "Sade, don't hit your brother."

"Can I hit her back, Mommy?"

"Did you like it when she hit you?"

"No!"

"Then don't hit her. Smart people fight with their words, not with their hands. Now, who would like a fruit cup?"

"Me! Mommy, me!" Nate was demanding, right in

her face. Like his dad.

"I would, please," Sade said politely. Like her mom.

Destiny read several messages, including one from Nate and another from Savannah, her personal assistant, and then stood to get the kids' treats. They sat at a table on one of three decks around their palatial home in Lake Las Vegas, one that both Nate and Destiny had helped design. At eighty-two degrees the temperature was rising but the patio covering and a misting system kept the trio comfortable. Just as they finished up and headed inside, the call Destiny had been anticipating came in. Best friend, TV host, preacher's daughter and basketball wife Princess Petersen was on the line.

Destiny had met Princess years ago, when she became involved with the Sanctity of Sisterhood conferences led by Princess's play aunt, Vivian Montgomery. Back then they'd been cordial, finding common ground in their close ages and interests. But it wasn't until Nate's scandal and Destiny's shame that the two became close. Princess had endured her own controversy and knew what it was like to be publicly judged. Her phone calls of support and subsequent visits to Turks and Caicos with her husband, Kelvin, elevated the women's relationship from casual associates to best friends.

"Hey, girl. Perfect timing. I'm just taking the kids to Meagan for their naps. Can you hold for a sec?" Destiny reached the great room and pushed a button. Meagan, the nanny, appeared within seconds and led the tired youngsters away. "Okay, I'm back. I'm headed to the suite so I can put you on speaker."

"Are you sure you want to do that?"

Destiny laughed. "Nate and I made sure that room

was soundproof. We'll be fine." She reached the suite, closed the double doors and sat in the large sitting room. "Okay, sis." She hit the speaker button and set down the phone. "Let's start with that game Saturday night. Your man did his thing!"

"You watched it?"

"As loud as Mark and Nate were, I might as well have. You'd have thought they had bets on the game or stock in NBA."

"Kelvin reserved tickets for them."

"I know. Nate told me. About a dozen times. Broke his heart not to use them."

"We held a drawing for his Twitter followers, fans who'd never get to a game on their own. The winners were thrilled. So let them know their sacrifice helped a worthy cause."

"Will do."

"Now, about the anniversary," she paused. "No, wait. Let's start with this Melody chick you mentioned yesterday."

"If you insist. We were good friends when I lived in Louisiana, and later Texas."

"Were?"

"Yes. Until she slept with Nate."

"She slept with your husband?"

"He wasn't at the time, but, yes, she slept with him."

"And she knew about the two of you?"

"Yep."

"Those are the worst."

"You'd think so, but it's even worse than that." A pause for effect and then, "she's the one in the video."

Princess gasped. "Shut. Up."

"I shared this before, on the island. That's why her name sounded familiar. Now you understand why I was grateful for your call. It stopped a line of questions that I didn't want to answer."

One word—video—and Destiny knew Princess would figure out who'd been met at the mall. Years earlier, a tape that was made without Nate's knowledge ended up in public view. What he'd been doing with the woman on the tape was less like preaching the gospel and more like laying on hands.

"Oh my God, Destiny."

"When I saw her you can just about imagine what all went through my mind."

"And God would have forgiven you for every transgression you put on her, might've even slapped you a high five."

"An altercation might have been satisfying, but it wouldn't have been worth it. Nate didn't crawl into her bed with a gun to his head. I couldn't put all the blame on her. Anyway, she lives here. In Vegas."

"Since when?" A strong vibe of suspicion accompanied the words.

Destiny managed a chuckle. "I thought the same thing. That she was back on the hunt. But she says she's been here for two or three years."

"Hmm. Who saw who first?"

"She saw me."

"And had the nerve to approach you and speak? That chick not only likes balls, she owns a pair."

"She's always been bold like that. It's how we became friends."

"Skanky side chicks are worse than roaches," Princess said with a sigh. "No matter how much insecticide you spray they keep coming back."

"Are we still talking about me? Or are we talking about you?"

"We're having a problem with Kelly, which means we're having a problem with Fawn."

They hadn't talked much about the woman who'd dated Princess's husband, Kelvin, in college and turned him into a baby daddy but Destiny definitely remembered the name.

"What's going on?"

"Something that might end up involving attorneys and child protective services."

"Oh, no. Is Kelly all right?"

"Kelvin doesn't think so. I think the boy is fine and that Fawn is up to her attention-grabbing tricks. I don't even have the energy to talk about that right now...trying to escape my problems by listening to yours."

"Ha! Glad I could help."

"Hey, that's what friends are for! Now back to Melody. Is she married?"

"No, but she has a steady man, or so she says."

"Good. Let her stay with him while you keep it moving. And whatever you do, don't invite her to church."

"Girl, please. As if I would! Although she did ask for the name and when she insinuated that I was insecure about her visiting, I sure enough told her." Princess groaned. "I doubt she'll come. But if she does I'll look at it as keeping my enemy closer."

"That's probably the best way to look at it. Speaking of enemies, how did things go with step-hoe?"

"Come on now, girl," Destiny chided. "That doesn't sound very Christian."

"Bitch doesn't sound Christian. For my father's messy wife, hoe is about the nicest I can do."

"I hear you," Destiny replied. "But what about

calling her Charmaine? That's her name."

"Why does it sound like you're on her side?"

"Because you're in your feelings. I'm on your side. And the side of what you know is right. At the end of the day, she's the mother of your half-brother and your father's wife."

"A half-brother who's two decades plus younger than me. Kiera is older than her uncle. That almost sounds illegal."

"On the other hand, think of how close the two will be. Your daughter and half-brother will grow up together."

"One big happy family, right? You sound like Kelvin, wanting to move his son in with us. Heck, do that and you might as well move in Fawn. I'm not even trying to hear that mess."

"I can understand your thoughts about Fawn but when it comes to Charmaine you could at least be cordial. You hardly see her anyway. Not liking her hurts you too, and puts distance between you and your dad. I know from experience how unproductive it is to harbor feelings about a situation outside of your control."

"Listen to you! Sounding all grown and first lady-like. You're definitely Lady Vivian's mentee."

"There are some things happening at Divine Grace that are too grown for me."

"Like what, another Melody?"

"No, thank God. I'll tell you later. We were talking about Charmaine."

"From the change in your voice her story can wait."

Destiny sighed softly. "The mere thought of talking about it makes me sick."

"Sounds serious."

"It could be." Destiny got up, grabbed a bottle of

sparkling water from the mini-fridge, and returned to the loveseat. "We've got a deacon who can't keep his dick to himself."

"Whoa!"

"And I think he's beating his wife."

"Double whoa!" Princess exclaimed. "Unfortunately, situations like that are happening in congregations all over the country. As a preacher's kid, I could tell you stories that you just can't make up."

Destiny thought of her own church experience and the Noble legacy. "Yes, I could share a story or two myself."

"So, he's sleeping with other women in the church?"

"In, out, my guess is wherever he can find a willing partner. He's behaved inappropriately with me so I can only imagine how he treats other women."

"You? What's he done to you?"

Destiny shared what had happened on Sunday, his constant staring and molesting her hand. "When we first arrived he'd make comments, teasing Nate about taking me from him and always commenting on my looks. It became uncomfortable and Nate shut it down. I don't know why he's back at it, but he is."

"What did Nate say?"

Destiny nervously bit her lip. "I haven't told him yet, not in detail"

"Destiny, you have to."

"I know, but Nate already doesn't care for the man. He was ready to kick his butt and kick him out of the church the last time this got out of hand. Now, with what I feel is going on in his marriage, I wouldn't want our reprimand used as an excuse to hit his wife."

"I understand, but you can't keep this a secret, Destiny."

"I know."

"I don't mean to stress you out even more than you are. Tell you what. If the team wins tonight, you and Nate attend game seven?"

"If they win? Don't you mean when?"

"Isn't that what I said?"

They laughed. "That's a very generous offer, Princess. Are you sure?"

"Absolutely."

"I can't believe you guys still have tickets. Your dad doesn't want to see the game live? Or Pastor Derrick?"

"Kelvin has already hooked them up. They're going to be in one of his sponsor's suites. Nate can join them there if he'd like. So…are you guys coming?"

"I'll check with Nate but can't imagine him saying no."

"Good. Once you confirm it, I'll send over your passes and arrange your travel. We'll set up a private plane to avoid the airport hassle."

"Look, I know you guys are balling but you don't have to do that."

"I know I don't have to. I want to."

"Thanks, Princess."

"Thank you, Destiny."

"For what?"

"For being a first lady as well as a true friend. You're right about Charmaine. I need to pray and ask God to change my heart toward her."

"I'll pray, too, not only about that but about seeing Melody."

"You need to pray about that so-called deacon and his nasty ways. And you need to tell Nate what happened. Girl, the other day when you said we needed an hour you didn't lie. We could have used two!"

"I know, right? I didn't even get to the matter of this year's SOS Conference, and I really want to hear about what's going on with Kelly and Fawn."

"Next time."

"Let's make it sooner rather than later."

"Sounds like a plan."

The two friends said their goodbyes and hung up. Destiny pondered Princess's advice to tell Nate the details about Ronald's renewed behavior. She couldn't help but imagine that not ending well. Hopefully, last Sunday was an isolated event and she could put it behind her. Which is what she hoped for Melody too, the other encounter she hadn't shared with him. She told herself there was no need, that the chances of Melody showing up at Divine Grace were slim to none. But a part of her felt that telling Nate about Melody might lead him into temptation, where being delivered from evil was not guaranteed.

6

Destiny believed in solving problems through prayer but Nate was leaning more toward the laying on of hands to handle the situation that bothered him this week. Not the kind that healed, but the kind in which the recipient would need healing. He forced thoughts of Ronald Miller out of his mind and focused on this Wednesday night's prayer and bible study. The irony of the night's lesson coming from 1 Corinthians 13, known to many as the love chapter, wasn't lost on him. God was trying to send a message. In Nate's current mood, good luck with that.

His right-hand man, Ben Harvey, knew his pastor and good friend was troubled and wanted to help. "Something's been bothering you all week. Do you want to talk about it?"

"Talking isn't exactly what I have in mind, although it's probably the better alternative."

Ben took a seat in front of Nate's desk, crossed one leg over the other and waited. As quiet and introspective as Nate was an extrovert, he'd been a steadying force in the multi-faceted pastor's life for five years, and knew Nate way better than some who'd known him longer. They'd met at a low point in Nate's life, before he became a nationally-known motivational speaker and bestselling author. Ben's ability to serve as a great listener and trustworthy confidante had given him entry into Nate's very small circle of close friends.

Nate put down the pen he toyed with and leaned back in the black leather swivel chair. "It's about Ron."

Ben nodded. "I'm not surprised."

"I didn't think you would be. You never cared for him much."

"I have a healthy respect for reptiles. But I hate snakes."

Nate smiled. "I'm not overly fond of him either, as you well know. I'd hoped that after you replaced Roy as the assistant pastor, he and Ron would leave the church."

"And give up their prominent positions and all the prestige? This is one of the fastest growing churches on the west coast right now. People from all over the country are coming to hear you, man."

"They're coming to see how the dead has arisen."

Years ago, the national scandal that set Destiny at such odds with Melody had cost Nate his ministry and, for a while, his reputation. He and his wife had moved—some would say fled—to Turks and Caicos. There they nursed his wounded ego and rebuilt his image. He'd written a self-help book which became a *New York Times* bestseller and opened the door to motivational speaking. A second book followed and was also well received. The expanded audience and book sales made Nate a multi-millionaire. A year ago Divine Grace invited him to preach a one-week revival, at least that's what the council of ministers had told him. In fact, it had been an unofficial evaluation, followed by an offer to become the church's senior pastor.

"However it's happening, people are coming through

the door in droves. The Word, the music and the power of God felt in each and every service keeps them coming back. Membership has exploded."

"Yes, which is what they were counting on, my popularity to bring in the masses. They had a negative bank account and knew that I could fill the pews."

"That's just what you did, and with middle and upper-income folk with healthy tithes. You changed the energy, brother. Now look at us. We need a bigger sanctuary and are getting ready to build it. And since Ron's company is one of the contractors under consideration, I definitely want to hear what's going on with him."

"You'd think a chance to make several hundred thousand dollars would keep a brother on the straight and narrow. But it appears he's back to his player ways."

"Who's he screwing now?"

"I don't know, but he's bothering Destiny."

Ben leaned forward, a frown on his face. "What do you mean, bothering her?"

"Destiny said it was the way he looked at her, you know, disrespectfully. But the way she acted on Sunday, after the program and on through the dinner, suggests it was more than that."

"She was quiet during dinner. During the drive home, Savannah commented on that."

"I'm going to put a stop to whatever he's doing. Tonight." Nate looked at his watch. Praise and worship was underway, which meant it was time for him to shed the protective husband mantle and slip into the teacher and preacher role. He reached for his iPad and stood.

The two men headed out of Nate's office into the larger executive offices where a few associate ministers and employees were also preparing to enter the sanctuary.

"Tell Ron I want to see him after bible study," Nate said, his voice lowered so that only Ben could hear.

Ben stopped while they were still several feet from the others present. "I'll deliver that message, but only if you promise me that talking is all you'll do."

Nate smiled at Ben. "Of course. You know me better than that."

"It's because I know you that I extracted the promise."

The two men laughed, joining the others in a circle for the pre-service prayer. The group of seven came through a side door and entered a sanctuary in the midst of praise and worship. The atmosphere was festive, the spirit high. It's what Nate needed—to focus on ministry and effectively talk about love.

Just under two hours later bible study ended, and moments after Nate returned to his office, there was a knock on his door.

"Enter."

The door opened. "You wanted to see me Reverend?"

"Sit down, Ron." Nate, sending a text to Destiny, who'd not been at church tonight, did not look up immediately. Even after finishing the text, he let several long, uncomfortable seconds tick by.

Ronald shifted in his seat. Nate glanced up at him. Ronald's eyes were fixed on a framed picture of Destiny sitting on Nate's desk. In the waist-up portrait, she looked appropriately respectful, wearing a cream-colored suit coat over a floral knit shell. Only he and Destiny knew that the impish grin and sparkle in her eyes was because she was naked from the waist down, body thrumming from what had happened on that chair just before the picture was snapped. But the way Ron was ogling at it, one would have thought he could see her shaved punanny. It made Nate want to punch him in the face. He told himself to chill. It had taken five years to get back into church ministry and they'd just celebrated their first year. To make headlines as a deacon-strangling minister wouldn't be a good look.

He set down the phone, and leaned back. "She's a beautiful woman, isn't she?"

"I've made no secret of what I think about your wife, Rev. Destiny is the most beautiful woman I've ever seen in my life." Ronald's eyes shifted from the picture to Nate. "You're a lucky man."

"I agree with you wholeheartedly. Lucky and blessed. I don't deserve a woman like her but God gave her to me anyway. I would lay down my life for my wife in a heartbeat, do everything in my power to keep her feeling safe and protected. That's why you're here."

A slight smirk crossed Ron's face. "Let me guess. You want me to be her bodyguard." A man facing execution couldn't have looked more serious than Nate right now. "I'm just joking, Rev."

"This is not a joking matter. I thought you'd put your disrespectful treatment of women behind you but I've been told that this is not the case."

"By whom?"

Nate ignored the question. "Does it matter?"

"It must have been the first lady. I admit I checked her out at the anniversary service, along with the other thousand or so people who were there. So what?"

"If you checked her out in the same way you just eyed that picture," Nate nodded toward the frame, "then it was totally inappropriate."

Ronald shrugged, and leaned back in the chair. "Can't blame a brother for looking, man."

Nate's back went ramrod straight, even as his countenance remained relaxed. "Excuse me?"

"Umm, I mean, Reverend. Sorry about that. I thought we were just talking man to man."

"I believe I'm beginning to see the problem we have here. For some reason, you view us as equals."

"It's not that, Rev—"

"I'm talking. Which means you shouldn't be." Ronald clenched his jaw, a signal to Nate that he was getting under the deacon's skin. "You have about fifteen or so years on me in age but spiritually, I am your elder. You will treat me with the respect and honor that I'm due, or you will find another church home. By extension, this respect and honor extends to my wife and family. Am I clear?"

"Yes, Reverend." He punctuated the last word with a devilish sneer.

"I know you and your brother have a long history at this church, and that your mother was one of its founding members. That is why I agreed to let you and Roy retain leadership positions for one year. During this time, there have been numerous occasions where your character and judgment have been called into question. As head deacon and a church leader, that isn't good for the ministry. It isn't good for me. I'm telling you now, in this fall's executive session, changes will be made."

All manner of joviality left Ronald's face. "Are you saying you're replacing a member who helped build this ministry, and can help take it to the next level?"

"Not yet. But you're being placed under careful scrutiny, an unofficial probation if you will, for the next ninety days. If I hear of any other type of impropriety or misconduct you will be immediately relieved of all duties and responsibilities."

"With all due respect, Reverend," he said with the face of one smelling chitterlings for the first time, "is that what happened to you?"

Nate steepled his fingers beneath his chin, his gaze at Ronald unflinching. "Regarding what, exactly?"

"We all know why you were MIA from ministry for the last five years. I'm assuming that the time you were caught with your pants not only down but off must have been your first time sinning, since you say I have no room for error."

"No man is without sin, deacon. I've missed the mark too many times to count, and before I'm called to meet my Maker will undoubtedly miss again. But we're not talking about me right now. We're talking about you, and what I feel is an inappropriate, ongoing attraction for this ministry's first lady.

"I'm only going to say this once. Whatever you're doing, stop. Whatever you're thinking, shut it down. If it takes not looking at her to keep your thoughts honorable, turn away. If your eye offends you, pluck it out. And not just her. This goes for all the women at Divine Grace. You think I don't know what you're about? You think it's a secret that you're bed hopping throughout the congregation? I've been there, Ronald—promiscuous, indiscriminate, uncaring. I'm not proud of it. I'm not judging. I'm saying that you need to either curtail the extracurricular activities happening outside your marriage or you will be sat down. Divine Grace is under new management and if you are not happy with how things are being run, perhaps you should consider a new church home."

"Divine Grace is just as much my church as it is yours. Maybe even more so. I'm not going anywhere."

"Then I'll assume there will be no more problems.

Besides, I'm not the only blessed man in this room. Janet is a lovely woman, godly, faithful. Wouldn't you agree that she deserves to be treated honorably, and with more respect?"

"When it comes to this ministry, I'll concede that you're the boss. But I'm the head of my wife and our household. I don't need your help in handling that."

"Prove it. I don't want to hear another word about your actions regarding Destiny or any other woman at this church. If I do, not only will your company be removed from consideration for the building contract but your membership at Divine Grace will be history. Is there anything about what I've just stated that you don't understand?"

"No, Reverend, you've been quite clear." If Ronald's face was made of stone, it could not have been more set.

"Good." Nate reached for his cell phone, and began to scroll. "Close the door on your way out."

7

Back in Lake Las Vegas, Destiny had received Nate's text about a meeting after service. Since he wouldn't be home for another hour she decided to return Simone's call from earlier.

"Hey, Mom. Returning your call."

"Home from church already?"

"I didn't go tonight. The last few weeks have been busy. I've hardly seen the kids so we spent the day together. I just tucked them in with a bedtime story. You know, Mommy stuff."

"I'm so proud of you, Destiny. You always knew what you wanted and while I thought you were way too young, marrying Nathaniel was the right thing for you. Had there been any remaining doubts, and there aren't, watching you this past weekend would have removed them."

"Thanks, Mom. Being married isn't always easy."

"Especially to a man like Nate." Simone was a couple years older than Nate. They'd grown up together in Palestine, Texas. Simone was very aware of Nate's magnetism with women and his prior reputation of handling several at once.

"So…why'd you call earlier?"

"Well, I've been inspired to write a song."

"Really? That's cool, Mom."

"We'll see how cool it is when I get finished. But so far I kind of like it."

"Have you written songs before?"

"Back in college I wrote a couple for a band I performed with on campus. Just a local thing. We were popular around town, but that's about it."

"I didn't know that."

"There's a lot about me that you don't know."

"True."

"You want to know what inspired me to write?"

"Sure."

"You."

"Me?"

"Indirectly. It's something Nate said at Sunday's dinner. He was talking about you guys and quality time, called it a date with destiny. There was a real ring to it."

"You got inspired by that cheesy line?"

Simone laughed. "I think it's adorable, the way he says that about you. When thinking about it later the phrase took on a deeper, more spiritual meaning. Our pastor frequently reminds us that there are no accidents in God's creation. That we're here for a reason, and that all of us have a date with whatever that reason is—that purpose or vocation or relationship or whatever we came into the earth to be and to do. We all have a date with destiny."

"Wow, that's beautiful, Mom. I believe that, too."

"I know you do. You believed it with Nate. No matter what Mom and I thought about your choice you believed he was your destiny, and somehow knew that being with him wasn't only about the two of you, but something greater that we've not yet seen. I didn't understand it, which was obvious by my staunch opposition. But you knew."

Destiny was silent for a moment, thinking back to that tumultuous time. She and her mother fought constantly about Nate. As the relationship rapidly progressed and Destiny needed advice it was Kat, not her mother, who was there to support her. That she had Simone's approval now was not taken for granted. "Yes, Mom. I knew. And I didn't even understand how I could be so sure of it. I was so young, had no real idea about love. But I felt the conviction of it deep in my heart."

"I remember how focused you were, through all of the women and the drama and the haters. You had a date with Nate. And not just with him, but with your joint mission to advance the kingdom of God. The same is true for Mark and me. It's a blessing to be his wife. I'd planned differently, but now it's clear that I was supposed to be by his side, as he occupied the position of governor for the state of Louisiana and now, as he grows his consulting business around the world. Of course we were also supposed to be the parents of our perfect child."

The women laughed. When it came to doting on young sons these two were neck and neck.

"None of us could see it at the time, but everything worked out exactly the way it was supposed to. The more I thought about this the more his statement stayed on my mind. Then a couple days ago more words started coming to me."

"So sing it for me. How does it go?"

"I don't have that much yet, just the chorus."

"Then sing that."

Simone cleared her throat and began to sing, her rich, silky voice floating from the speaker.

"I have a date with destiny."

I'm going to get all God has for me.

Got no time for drama, please don't take it personally.

I have a date with destiny."

"I hear that!" Destiny exclaimed. "No time for drama. Amen!"

"So you like that chorus?"

"I love it, Mom. Can't wait until it's finished."

"Me, either. Look, sweetie, Mark is calling me. I have to go."

"Okay. Thank you for sharing what you said tonight. I needed to hear that."

"Is something going on, Destiny?"

"The usual. Church stuff, mainly."

"Destiny. You should know better than to think you can fool your mother. Is this about that girl you saw when we were out shopping?"

Genuine surprise registered on Destiny's face. "Why would you think it's about her?"

"Because you tried to downplay the meeting when disgust and irritation were all over your face."

"You saw that, huh?"

"Yes, I did."

Destiny let out a resigned sigh. "It was Melody Anderson, Mom. The girl in the video."

"What video?" Destiny remained quiet, waiting for the lightbulb to turn on. "Wait...*tha*t video? No!"

"Yes."

"That was her?"

"Sure was. And worse than running into her was finding out she lives here in Vegas."

"Oh my God." A pause and then, "does Nate know?"

"No, and I'm not telling him either. But not because I feel threatened, which is what Melody believes."

"She told you that?"

"She insinuated there were problems in my marriage when I hesitated to give her the name of our church."

"Jesus, Destiny. What are you going to do?"

"Exactly what I need to do. Nothing. Melody Anderson is in my rear-view mirror, and I'm not putting my life in reverse."

The call ended, and not long afterward, Nate came home. Conversation was limited. Both had a lot on their minds. For Nate, it was Destiny and the continued nagging feeling that there were secrets between them. For Destiny, it was Nate and the secrets between them. As she drifted off to sleep, though, it was to the memory of her mom singing on the phone.

No time for drama, please don't take it personally. I have a date with destiny.

Destiny indeed believed God had more in store for her, Nate, the ministry, their family. She just wondered how much drama she'd have to wade through to get to it, and if she was strong enough to survive.

8

It was the Thursday before the weekend of game seven in the championship playoffs. Whoever won tonight was headed to the NBA finals. Kelvin and the team wanted so badly to win. Princess was both excited and nervous, which is why she was even more grateful than usual that her mother was in town for a visit. As a teenager, she and Tai Brook had gone a few rounds. But now as an adult wife, mother and career woman, the two had become best friends.

She looked up and smiled as Tai brought two mugs of steaming hot chocolate, Princess's childhood favorite into the dining room. "Every time you come here I tell you not to do this. You're obviously not listening." She accepted the mug. "Thanks."

"And I keep telling you that I'm the mom, you're the daughter." Tai Brook sat, placed her mug on a coaster and reached for the tray of pastries in front of her. "You're not listening, either. Where's Kiara?"

"With Bella."

"You'd better hope that child doesn't develop more affection for her nanny than her mother."

"There's no chance of that happening. I know it seems that she's always with her, but that's because the last few times you've been here there's been so much going on. Like the championship tournament, for instance."

Tai laughed. "Point taken."

"Trust me, Kiara knows I'm her mama. We won't get that twisted."

"Considering all you went through, I'm sure that's a title you'll not easily relinquish."

Princess nodded, her eyes dimmed.

Tai reached out and squeezed her daughter's hand. "It's still hurts, huh?"

Princess nodded. "Probably always will."

"I can't explain why what happened happened honey. But God doesn't make mistakes."

The two women quietly sipped hot chocolate, their thoughts transported back to what happened three months into Princess's pregnancy. She'd been expecting twins. One miscarried. Princess had been beside herself with guilt. How could that happen? What had she done? The doctor had assured her that what occurred had been nature's way of handling an improperly developing embryo. "Vanishing child syndrome" is the phrase he'd used, though neither Tai nor Princess had ever heard of it before. Counselors had encouraged her to focus on the healthy child still growing inside her. Princess doted on Kiara. The sun rose and set on that child. But she would never forget the second heartbeat detected in that first ultrasound, the one she fervently believed belonged to the son she'd prayed for, the son who was her angel now.

Tai rested against the chair as she set down her mug. "When is King getting here?"

"Not until tomorrow afternoon. And he's leaving on Saturday."

"Quick trip."

"I'm surprised he's coming at all." At Tai's questioning look, she continued. "Charmaine wanted to come too."

"Oh."

"You knew that wasn't happening. From what I hear, she and that son of hers could use the bonding time. If anyone grows up not knowing his mama it will be him."

"And you say that because?"

"According to Tabitha, nine times out of ten that child is either with her or the nanny. Daddy's always focused on church business, as usual, and Charmaine is always out."

Tai's brow raised as she leaned against the seatback. "Out where?"

Princess shrugged. "Dining. Shopping. The gym, where Tabitha says she works out with this fine hands-on personal trainer almost every morning."

"Tabitha would know. Your baby sister is worse than TMZ. I had to finally tell her to stop with the play-by-play." The women laughed. "Hands-on, huh? I wonder if she's…"

"Don't know, don't want to know. It's none of my business."

"Mine either." Tai took another thoughtful sip. "But it would be fitting justice for King to get a taste of the medicine I swallowed for twenty-plus years." She reached for a croissant and enjoyed a bite. "Cute little boy, though. I saw your picture of him and Kiara together. No way could King deny him. Looks just like him and Daddy O."

Princess picked up a pastry, placed it on her saucer and began picking off and nibbling the frosting. "I still can't believe we're living the ghetto life. My daughter's uncle is only a few years younger than she is!"

"You think you were shocked? I was floored, knew that girl was lying just to get King to marry her."

"But then the blood test came back ..."

"And it was proven that King was part of the two percent of men who have a child after having a vasectomy. He always did have strong swimmers."

"Mom, there are some things about Daddy that I don't need to know."

"Wait! That's who's missing."

"Who?"

"Where's Kelly? I just knew he'd be here this weekend."

Princess let out an exasperated breath and put down her mug. "We haven't seen Kelvin's son for the past three weeks."

"Why not? Did you guys change the schedule?"

"We didn't. Fawn did."

At the sound of Fawn's name, Tai got an immediate attitude. About the only thing she hated worse than Kelvin and Princess dating in college was the hurt Fawn caused her daughter when trying to tear them apart.

"What the hell is she doing?"

"That's what we're trying to figure out. Kelvin says that something's going on with Kelly, that the last time he was here he wasn't himself. He was sullen and withdrawn. He's always a bit quieter with me so I didn't notice it so much. But it bothered Kelvin enough for him to call Fawn and ask what was going on. In typical fashion she went off, screaming and cursing as if he'd accused her of something, which he hadn't. He's just a concerned father trying to find out what's wrong with his son."

"Do you have any idea what it could be?"

"I wouldn't put it past Fawn to be instigating a situation just to get Kelvin's attention. She's messy like that. But we do know that she recently moved her new dude into the house, the one she's only been dating a few months. So he's probably trying to adjust to that, no longer being man of the house."

"That could be it. Little boys can be protective of their mamas."

"Right."

"What do you know about this guy? The new boyfriend."

"Not much. Kelvin talked to Fawn's cousin but she didn't could only tell him that his name was Gerald and that he had two kids. Oh, and that he was trying to be about that thug life."

"Good Lord."

"After more than a week of trying and not getting any answers or a returned phone call, Kelvin told his accountant to hold Fawn's next check. Stopping her money will lead to a phone call, believe that."

"You'd think a condo, car and five-thousand a month would be enough to make her happy and want to act right."

"Oh, no. She's complained about that measly amount of money since this whole thing started. She wanted ten, and that's after Kelvin bought her a condo, leased her a new car and took over the household expenses."

"Kelvin's got to be too through with that girl."

"He's frustrated, and really worried about Kelly. I told him to focus on work until after the playoffs. We'll figure it all out after that."

After another quiet moment, Tai changed the subject. "Didn't you say your bestie is joining you at the game this weekend?"

Princess nodded, more than happy to change the subject. "Both she and Nate will be there."

"Is King staying here?"

"Where else would he stay?"

"A hotel, preferably."

"A ten-thousand-square-foot house isn't big enough for the two of you?"

Tai looked properly trite. "I guess you could tie a bell on his shoe or something, so I'll know when he's coming and go the other direction."

"Ha! Charmaine's not going to be with him. It won't be that bad."

"I guess not."

"I know I'm grown and it shouldn't matter but it will be nice to see my parents together, for a change."

"You say that as if he and I don't get along. I was just kidding about the bell. I'm not mad at King anymore. I've forgiven him for what happened during our marriage. Now, I'm just trying to be happy and live my life."

"Are you happy, Mom?"

Tai slowly nodded. "I'm getting there. That beautiful grandbaby of mine helps a lot."

"Speaking of," Princess began, looking at her watch and standing up. "Kiara should be awake from her nap by now. You want to go spoil her?"

"Of course. That's my primary reason for being here."

The two ladies linked arms and headed down the hall toward the children's wing. "It's good to have you here, Mom."

"It's good to be here, Princess."

"I love you."

"Love you more. Give the situation with Kelly over

to God. He knows what's going on and can fix it. Don't let Fawn's dealings with Kelvin ruin your weekend. Women chasing your husband can add years to your life. And I'm not talking about what I heard, but what I know."

9

Destiny parked her car in the spot reserved for "The First Lady." At first she'd balked at the title. Especially when called that by those old enough to be her mother, or grandmother. But Vivian Montgomery had encouraged her to walk with confidence in the position and authority that God had given her. She'd further explained that the title was a sign of distinction and respect. To be successful in the position, Vivian assured her, she'd need both.

Her mentor was right. Even the title was sometimes not enough to get due respect. Ronald Miller's actions last Sunday had proven that. Princess was right, too. Nate needed to know the whole story. But, later, Destiny decided. After their trip to Phoenix and the playoff game. The past few months had been hectic and now that the church was moving forward on plans for a new building it would likely not slow down soon. Nate tried not to bring the stress from work into their home but when her man was troubled, Destiny knew.

Like last night, for instance. When Nate returned from mid-week worship and bible study, he was perturbed. She'd asked what was bothering him and was told it was nothing for her to worry about. He'd spent over an hour in his office before coming to bed. Destiny knew how to change his focus. When he came to bed she was wearing an edible thong, and after licking his shaft like an ice cream cone, asked if he was hungry. The man was starved. By the time he'd fallen into slumber an hour later, the tenseness in his shoulders had finally loosened. This morning, the memory of last night's acrobatics were etched on her sore thighs. It was a pain that she relished. Happy man, great marriage plan.

She used her key to open the private side entrance and was surprised when Savannah, her personal assistant, met her in the foyer.

"Good morning, Savannah."

"Good morning, Lady."

"Why are you here in the foyer, lying in wait? Am I late for a meeting?"

She started for the hallway, but Savannah stayed her with a hand on her forearm. "You've got a visitor," she responded, her voice just above a whisper.

"Okay," the word drawn out by the knowledge that there was more to the story.

Savannah looked around. The hallways were empty. "It's Janet Miller," she whispered, then quickly put a finger to her lip signaling for quiet. Destiny didn't see anyone around. Did Savannah think the wall had ears?

The two women proceeded down the hall, both silent and praying. They arrived at the reception area outside her office. "Hold my calls," Destiny said as they entered. "And please prepare a tea cart with fresh fruit and bagels."

"Right away."

Destiny walked over to her office door and placed a hand on the knob. She bowed her head and closed her eyes. *Holy Spirit, I need you. Let me hear this dear sister with a heart of compassion. Help me counsel with grace. I don't what she's going through, but, Father, You know. Please help me. Thank you. Amen.* After a last calming breath, she put a slight smile on her face and opened the door.

"Good morning, Janet."

"Morning, Lady."

One look at Janet Miller and Destiny's pleasant expression disappeared, replaced by one of concern. Janet wore large, round sunglasses. Her bottom lip looked puffy. There was a scratch on her cheek that hadn't been there on Sunday. Janet had obviously been dealt another bad hand.

Destiny placed her briefcase and purse on the desk and sat in the chair next to Janet, who perched on the chair's edge with her head averted. Destiny remained quiet, waiting for Janet to take the lead. Within seconds, a lone tear escaped the confines of her keep-the-shame-a-secret shades. Acting instinctively, Destiny placed a hand on Janet's shoulder and begin to softly recite the 23rd Psalm.

"The Lord is my shepherd. I shall not want.

He maketh me to lie down in green pastures.

He leads me beside the still waters. He restores my soul."

Destiny paused, feeling a tiny bit of the tension dissipate from Janet's rigid shoulders. "The Word is powerful," she whispered, giving her shoulder a squeeze. "The power of life is in your tongue, my sister. Speaking the word can give you strength."

Janet remained quiet. Destiny continued.

"He leadeth me in the path of righteousness for his namesake."

"Yea though I walk through the valley of the

shadow of death," she said, a soft smile appearing as Janet's voice—soft and trembling—joined in.

"I will fear no evil. For Thou art with me."

Destiny stopped them. "Say it again."

Janet's shoulders trembled as she took a breath. "I will fear no evil. For Thou art with me."

"Who is Thou?" Destiny kept her voice low, but firm.

"God."

"I will fear no evil because God is with me. Say it."

"I will fear no evil because God is with me."

"Janet, do you believe that?"

Janet nodded.

"Say it again. Believe that God is with you and there is no one to fear."

A tear fell down Janet's face, chased by another. "I can't say that."

"Why not?" Destiny spoke in a near-whisper, while slowing rubbing her hand across shoulder blades that were tightening up again.

"I will fear...no evil because...God..." She clenched her jaw, her bottom quivered. Her hands were clasped tightly in her lap, as tears flowed.

"Lady," she managed, between quivering lips, "I do fear evil. I live with evil." She slowly removed the sunglasses and stared at her first lady through two black eyes. Destiny's hand went to her mouth. She recovered quickly, swallowing the gasp that threatened to escape and steeling her face into a look of compassion instead of one reflecting the horror she felt. "I'd run to the devil to escape Ron Miller. Evil is too good a word to describe him. If he finds out I'm..."

"He won't. I promise. You're safe here."

Finally, the dam of restraint broke, and Janet along

with it. It seemed getting through the night and coming here this morning had taken all of her strength. She fell into Destiny's arms.

"It's okay, sister." Destiny hugged her, as her eyes misted. "Go ahead and cry."

A knock at the door and Janet froze. Her body began to shake uncontrollably. "It's him," she hissed, half-rising from her seat to flee but frightened into paralysis and unable to move. "I parked down the street, but he must have—"

"Janet. Listen! Listen to me." Destiny gripped Janet's arms, looked into fear-filled eyes. "It's not Ronald. It's Savannah, bringing the tea I requested. Okay?"

Janet nodded, and slipped the sunglasses back on. Savannah and Destiny made the exchange with nothing more than eye contact and a nod, but the text Destiny received moments after taking the tea cart into the small meeting room beyond her office let her know that her assistant, prayer partner and friend had picked up on the silent, spirit-sent request. Ronald Miller was not on church grounds. Janet was safe. For now.

Destiny fixed two cups of lemony chamomile and took them over to the table where Janet now sat.

Janet took a sip and winced as the hot liquid touched the split on her lip. "No, it's okay," she said as Destiny reached for a small ice bucket on the tray. "It's good and hot. I like it."

Destiny took a sip of her tea. For a few seconds, they drank in silence, then she set down her cup. "This is probably going to be a difficult conversation. But I need you to tell me what happened. I need to know how long Deacon Miller has been beating you up."

10

Something was wrong. Nate knew it as soon as he opened the door. Could feel it, almost taste it. This heightened level of intuition had been passed on to him by his mother, Nettie. His was nowhere near as keen as the woman who could tell you what color panties you'd be wearing on which day of the week, and sometimes appeared to fail him altogether. But when he was attuned to it, like now, it was unmistakable and accurate.

He walked along the quiet halls of a home that could be featured in an upscale magazine on architecture or interior design—past the large, two-story living area with floor to ceiling windows welcoming in the mountainous view. Past the formal dining room with its custom table for twelve made of ebony wood, steel, tempered glass and crystal inlays surrounded by silk-covered chairs. Past the entry to the gourmet kitchen where the subtle smell of something delicious being prepared by their full-time chef teased his nose. Through the great room with its dual-sided fireplace and pristine view of the magical Vegas Strip far below and down another hall to the children's play room where he finally heard voices.

He reached the doorway and for a moment just

stood there and gazed upon his treasure. His beautiful wife and the mother of his children, looking almost like one herself with her hair in a ponytail and one of his large t-shirts reaching mid-thigh as she sat cross-legged playing with Sade, their three-year-old daughter. Close by was his mini-me, Daniel Nathaniel, named after his grandfather and father and whom they also called Danny; he was playing a video game on the tablet he'd received for his fifth birthday. Nate had given up dozens of women to have this one in his life. Walking into the room, he realized he would have given up a thousand more.

"Daddy!" Sade jumped up and ran to her hero, wrapping her arms around his legs at the knee.

Nate picked her up, held her over his head and turned them both around. "How's my princess?"

Laughing she replied, "Fine, but you're making me dizzy!"

He kissed her cheek, put her down and walked over to Destiny, who now stood waiting. "Hey, baby."

"Hey."

Nate went in for a simple hug but found himself wrapped in a tight embrace. He pulled back and looked at her. "You all right?"

She gave him a light kiss. "Better now."

He put his hands on the sides of her face, looked deep into her eyes. "How are you?"

"Tell you later."

Nate turned to his son, still absorbed in his game. "Son." No answer. Nate took a step closer. "Son." Still nothing.

"Hmm, self-absorbed," Destiny murmured. "Wonder who he gets that from?"

Nate cut her a side-eye and walked over to pick up

his son. "Hello, young man."

"Hi, Daddy. I want to play my game."

"More than you want to talk to me?" The child nodded. "All right then, dude," he said, lowering Daniel to the floor. "Excuse me for interrupting. I only bought the game and the room you're playing it in but...my bad."

Daniel ignored him. Destiny chuckled.

He looked at her. "Heard you were at church today."

"I'm there every Thursday."

"Yes, but you didn't come by my office. You're slipping, woman."

"A last minute appointment got added to the schedule. I left as soon as the last one was over to be here in time for the conference call about this year's SOS conference."

"Next month, right?"

Destiny nodded. "And you won't believe what she asked me."

"What?"

"To speak at the final service on Saturday night."

"Baby, that's great!"

"Great? It's horrible! I'm not a speaker."

Nate wrapped his arms around her and pressed his groin against her flesh. "Don't worry, baby. I've got you. I'll teach you everything you need to know."

She swatted at his chest, then sat on the couch. "Public speaking isn't something you pick up in a month."

Nate followed, and sat beside her. "Why'd she wait so late to ask you?"

"Because the person who was originally scheduled just canceled. Lady Viv said it was Divine Order because the board is trying to encourage more young women to attend. I suggested she ask Princess. She's a talk show host who speaks in front of audiences all the time."

Nate shrugged. "That makes sense. Why not ask her?"

"She spoke last year. I promised to give it serious thought. And I'm thinking about seriously saying no."

"Come on, baby. I've never known you to run from a challenge."

"Let me check on dinner." She walked away thinking about what Nate said, and knowing that a speaking engagement isn't the only thing she wanted to run from right about now.

Later, after dinner had been eaten and the kids went away with the nanny for baths and bed, Destiny and Nate settled on the patio in matching lounge chairs. It was a balmy night, but the virgin daiquiris and cooling sprayer system that surrounded them kept them nice and comfy.

"Okay, baby," he said, reaching for her hand. "Out with it." He thought she'd stall but instead she swung her legs off the lounger and sat on the side. Her seriousness caused him to sit up, too.

"Nathaniel…"

"Uh, oh. This must be serious. You rarely call me by my full name."

"It's very serious, babe. What I'm about to share with you is in strict confidence, okay? You'll want to react. You'll want to do something. But you have to promise me that you won't. It's the only way I can share it."

He looked at her a long moment.

"Please, Nate."

"Okay."

"Janet was one of my appointments today, the unexpected one that we squeezed into the schedule." Destiny unconsciously chewed her bottom lip, thinking that there was no good way to discuss a bad thing.

"Go on."

"Ronald beat her up last night."

Nathan shifted his eyes away from her. He was sure they looked murderous, something his wife didn't need to see. "She told you?"

"She showed me."

"She had bruises?"

"I took pictures. For evidence. They're on the phone in my room."

"That lowdown motherfucker." When angry, this reverend was known to reach back for a curse word or two. "I'm relieving him of his duties tomorrow."

"Nate, you can't."

"Watch me."

"Nate," Destiny placed her hand on his. "Was it Ronald who you met with last night?"

Nate stilled, slowly sat back, as if the air had been punched from his lungs. "Yes, I did."

"She said that he didn't come home until about two this morning, and he'd been drinking. He accused her of putting their business in the street. She denied it. He beat her for talking, and again for lying. What did you say to him?"

"Nothing that warranted him kicking Janet's ass." Nate stood and paced. His movements resembled a panther on the prowl, searching for his prey. "I talked to him about you, Destiny, and the respect he should..." Nate stopped in his tracks. "Oh my God."

"What?"

"I told him that as his wife, Janet deserved his respect. Do you think that is what set him off?"

"Janet said anything can make him snap. It could have been that or something totally different. But she's afraid, Nate. She feels trapped, doesn't know what to do. He threatens her. Fear is how he controls. That's why you can't say anything. We can't let on that we know, at least not right now."

"I've got to fix this. It's my fault."

Destiny stood and walked over to Nate. "It is not your fault," she said sternly. "Nate, look at me." He did, eventually. "Ronald Miller is a grown man. You are not responsible for his actions. This abuse has been going on for years. As long as they've been together. Even before they were married."

"Well, something's got to happen, because I'm not going to let a wife-beater work in the ministry. Not only a deacon, whose charge is to set a Godly example, but the head deacon? And the director of finance? I'll be damned if that happens. There's no way."

"I know it's hard to do nothing. I'm frustrated, too. But we're not in that home. Janet is. She begged me not to tell anyone, and is terrified of Ronald finding out. If he beat her for thinking she talked to somebody, imagine what will happen if he learns she actually did?

"He checks her phone, so I bought her one of those temporary ones, the kind you can't track, so if necessary she'll have a way to contact me or someone outside of the home without his knowledge. Of course, I told her she should leave him, that no woman deserved to be abused."

"So why doesn't she?"

"The same reason that thousands of other abused women don't leave. Because she fears him, and loves him."

"What about Roy or his wife, Bethany? Maybe we can talk to them, get them to intervene. Or Janet's family, a sibling, somebody. Anybody who can say something where Ronald won't suspect his wife of talking."

"I asked the same question. But the people you mentioned have tried, over and over, and gave up on helping her a long time ago. Right now the only person I can think to call is Jesus."

Nate reached for her hands. "Then let's pray, Destiny. But just know that if we don't hear a quick answer from God that arrogant wife-beating bastard is going to have to answer to me."

"While you're praying, I might as well give you one more name to add to the list."

"Who?"

"Melody Anderson."

Nate's look was all kinds of WTF. "Why in the world would I put that woman's name across my lips?"

"Because she very well could come across your path. Or down an aisle in our church. She's here. In Las Vegas."

"Who told you that?"

"I ran into her last week."

"And you're just now telling me?"

"I'd rather not have told you at all. I'd rather have forgotten the incident happened and wished her away to a different city. A different planet would have been even better. She asked for the name of our church. I didn't want her to surprise you one Sunday by walking in and have you lose your Holy Ghost."

"I lost my ministry and reputation partly due to that girl. Trust and believe me when I tell you, I don't plan to lose anything else."

The two joined hands and petitioned God for grace, guidance, mercy and protection. Both knew He was more than able to do all they'd asked, but went to bed wondering how crazy life would begin to look before their prayer was answered.

11

Janet looked in the mirror, carefully studying her face. It had been less than twenty-four hours since the beating but by using tried and true methods to reduce pain, swelling and discoloration, her image had improved. Ice had reduced the swollen lip. A combination of antibiotic ointment, Vitamin E oil and tea tree oil had removed the redness from around the scratches that came from her vain attempts to dodge Ronald's blows. Alternate applications of a cold ice pack and crushed pineapple, every ten minutes almost all day, plus mega-doses of Vitamin C, had lessened the swelling around her eyes. She still looked like a raccoon's cousin, but five minutes with MAC's full long-wear concealer and full coverage foundation would have her ready to greet the world as the quiet, dutiful wife of the successful, handsome contract-company owner, Ronald Miller. It was a position many women envied, and wanted to fill. If they only knew. Janet longed to give them exactly what they wanted. If she could only gain the strength and the courage to walk away.

She reached for the face cleanser and a washcloth, and began methodically scrubbing her skin. Instead of the forty-five-year-old woman standing before the mirror, Janet stared into the face of the teenager who'd first laid eyes on a tall, strapping twenty-two-year-old Ronald Miller thirty years ago.

The date? 1985. The place? St. Louis, Missouri. Janet was the shy, sheltered, only daughter of Mr. and Mrs. Albert Rutherford, who'd been blessed with the child they never imagined would come from Mrs. Rutherford's forty-seven year old womb. Her parents were strict and overly protective. When Janet ran into the worldly Ron Miller, she'd never had a boyfriend. Never been kissed.

Ronald Miller soon changed all that.

At first he was a knight in shining armor, coming to rescue her from a group of teasing boys. Janet wasn't one of the prettier girls. She had a short Jherri curl, a pudgy figure, and acne. Her mother insisted on buying her clothes and refused to let her wear the punky, funky fashions made popular by celebrities like Madonna and Salt-n-Peppa, and shows like Soul Train and Fame. Janet wanted to dress like *The Cosby Show* girls. Her mother's choices were better suited for *Little House on the Prairie.* This didn't seem to matter to Ronald. He told her that he liked her smile, and bought her some cream to use on her face. It helped to clear up the acne. Over the next eighteen months, motivated to health and exercise by her newly found friend, Janet lost twenty pounds. Shortly after that she lost her virginity. But the real end to her innocence came three months later, the first time Ronald hit her. The reason? He accused her of flirting. The boy she'd spent time with was her cousin, and just thirteen years old.

With a makeup sponge and just the right amount of pressure, Janet carefully applied the concealer and made her black eyes disappear. Would that the violence in her first and only relationship had ended as quickly.

Of course, he was sorry, remorseful even. Swore that it would never happen again. Took her to his newly-rented apartment and placed her in bed, brought ice packs and flowers and later, loved all the hurt away. From this incident, Janet learned to be very careful with how she interacted with other men and, if possible, to not engage with them at all.

He wanted to be with her all the time and if not, to know where she was and who she was with. Because of how much he loved her. Because she was his world. This is what he told her. The close relationship she'd enjoyed with her parents became strained. They didn't like Ronald's attitude or how he treated Janet. What he defined as protection, her parents called control. They demanded, then requested, then begged Janet to stop seeing him. But she wouldn't.

Almost a year passed before the second act of violence occurred, during which time Janet fell even more in love with Ronald. He'd introduced her to sex but because of her conservative upbringing had kept the act to the basic missionary position. This all changed on her seventeenth birthday when he forced her to have anal sex. She'd refused at first, and been slapped senseless. As she cowered on the couch, Ronald towered over her and expressed that the classmates who'd teased her had been right. That nobody would want her but him, that it was because of her inferiority that he dated other women. He explained that if she loved him, she'd do what he wanted.

She loved him, and did.

Reaching for the foundation and a clean sponge, Janet recalled the first time she tried to leave Ronald. Her father died suddenly, of a massive heart attack, and the dose of reality hit her squarely in the face. The day after graduating high school, she'd left home and moved in with Ron. This basically meant she became his prisoner, having to answer to the five W's—who, where, when, what, why—at all times. There was little contact with her parents. She had no friends and little interaction with her co-workers. But on that rainy day in the cemetery, looking at the dark wooden coffin being lowered into the ground, Janet realized her life was no longer her own. And she wanted it back.

That weekend, while Ronald was at a party, she gathered her clothes and what other possessions would fit into a suitcase and moved back home with her mother. Within days, shards of her true self began to peek through the clouds. She fixed herself up, began wearing the makeup that Ronald forbade, and for a couple days actually thought she looked cute. She started going to church with her mother, something she hadn't done since leaving home. Six weeks later, Ronald showed up outside her job—tears in his eyes, black box in his hand. Her mind screamed no, but her mouth said yes. Two weeks later Janet Rutherford stood in a judge's chamber at the courthouse and became Mrs. Janet Miller. That night Ronald told her he owned her. That mind, body and soul, she belonged to him. For the next twenty-five years he accused, misused, berated and beat her into believing that this was true.

And now, as Janet stared into the perfectly made up face devoid of scars, ready to meet Ronald at a Chamber of Commerce dinner, she doubted it was possible to undo a lie that had lasted this long.

*

Ronald pulled his car into a vacant spot just steps away from where the Chamber dinner was being held. He looked in the mirror and straightened his silk, designer tie, making sure the black diamond tie stud was properly centered and that the matching cufflinks were turned just right. Examining his left and right profile, he admired his barber's handiwork, and wondered whether or not he should dye his hair or keep the subtle strands of gray coming in from being noticed. The woman he bedded earlier said they made him look distinguished. He checked his watch. Fifteen minutes before Janet was set to arrive. She knew to be on time, or there would be consequences. The chamber president's wife's affinity for her and his interest in obtaining a seat on the chamber board were the only reasons he'd invited her in the first place. That and the fact that he needed to present the image of a successful, happily married businessman to help hide the disorganized, debt-ridden, floundering company at bankruptcy's door. Now that Nate had threatened his positions as head deacon and director of finance at Divine Grace, which probably meant his chance of getting the building contract was also in jeopardy, the board member position had increased in value.

Thoughts of Nate and last night's meeting almost put a damper on what so far had been a stellar day. A job finished ahead of schedule had led to a five-figure bonus, part of which he'd spent on a pair of buxom brunette twins who were game for his proclivities. That the money should have gone to pay past due company bills wasn't even considered. His mind was on sex, and the woman with whom he most desired to share his kinky bed was married to the man he most hated. He'd never wanted Nate Thicke to become his pastor. His presence at Divine Grace had put a crimp in his lifestyle. That the man thought he could tell him how to run his own household was fifty shades of wrong. What he needed to be doing was making sure that fine-ass wife of his didn't get stolen right out from under him. She treated him coolly, but Ronald knew that was an act perpetuated to keep Nate happy. He'd probably smacked that ass a time or two to make her comply. But he'd seen her, staring. Checking him out. Probably wanting him as much as he did her. Ronald knew that given the right opportunity he could slap that bitch off her high horse, use his tool to turn her out and leave her begging for more.

*

Ronald had always had a way with women. From the time the babysitter seduced him when he was seven, until now, his dick had been a better weapon than any kind of gun. In the early days, a few got by him—the smart, fearless, confident ones. By the time he'd met Janet, however, he'd learned how to hunt the perfect prey. Now, he could pick them out on sight. Five seconds and he knew whether or not a woman was the type that could be dominated. Janet was one of the first ones with whom he'd tested this theory. She was also the prototype used to perfect the methods to keep a female weak and willing. Any abuse that Janet or any other woman received had been their own fault. It's what his father had told his mother when giving her a beating and the same logic applied when using an extension cord, leather belt or fists to discipline Ronald. His dad made sure the family knew that without him, his wife and son would be nothing. At the time Ronald rebelled against such nonsense, but not long into their relationship told

Janet the very same thing.

Ten minutes before the hour, Ronald watched his wife's white Hyundai Sonata with silver trim pull into the parking lot. He'd purchased the car six months ago, thought it looked like the type of car that his wife should be driving. This wife, anyway. If Destiny was his woman, he'd buy her a Lexus or Mercedes, top of the line. When Janet exited her vehicle, Ronald got out as well. He gave her a careful once-over, satisfied that her hair and makeup were flawless, and the designer suit and shoes exuded class and grace.

"Do I look okay?" she asked when she reached him.

He glanced at her and replied, "You're walking next to me. What do you think?"

He entered the building with Janet on his arm but with Destiny still on his mind. The more he fantasized about a night with the first lady, the more he wanted to make the dream come true.

12

Nate couldn't sleep. He tossed and turned, filled with anger, wracked with guilt. Destiny was right. The person to blame for Janet's abuse was her husband. Nate knew this, intellectually. But in his heart he felt guilty. Despite the judgment his family had received for the way they lived back in Palestine, Texas, and regardless of how they'd taught the word at Gospel Truth church, his father and grandfather had instilled in him to have the utmost respect for women. They'd said a man who hit a woman was lower than a dog with rabies, and that only a weak man would do so. Now, Nate was faced with a church member guilty of what the men in his family most reviled, the latest attack perhaps sparked out of anger about something Nate said. How could he possibly keep the promise to his wife and not confront Ronald? There was no way Nate could let him remain in the head deacon position, standing before the church as a righteous man when in truth he wasn't honorable at all. When the clock on the nightstand read four a.m. with Nate still awake, he eased out of bed and went outside. The night was clear. The sky held a thousand stars. Nate looked past the beauty of the night to the ugliness of man and again called on God.

"Lord God in heaven, I know I've prayed. My wife has prayed. I'm sure Janet has prayed. But my heart is still heavy. I'm frustrated, angry. I feel guilt for something that isn't my fault. No woman deserves to be beaten, and Janet least of all. She's a good woman; faithful, loyal. As her spiritual covering, I feel that she is my responsibility."

She's not your responsibility, but Mine.

Hearing from God through his inner voice stilled Nate's prayer. He knew the words were true but still felt conflicted. Since Janet was God's child, why didn't He protect her? Where was God when she was getting knocked upside the head?

Son, I was right there. Had I not been, she would be dead.

It was a rare thing for Nate to cry, but he felt his eyes begin to water. "My hands are tied, Father God. But Yours are not. I don't know how to right this situation, but You do. I'm going to stand in faith, and on Your word, and believe in my dear sister's deliverance from this pit of hell. Come quickly, Lord. He's got to be dealt with. In Jesus name."

Nate's talk with Jesus eased his soul enough to catch an hour or so of sleep. At six o'clock, he burned off more anxiety in their state-of-the-art home gym. He showered and dressed quietly, careful not to wake Destiny, who'd also slept fitfully but now seemed to sleep soundly. After making quick work of an egg white omelet with spinach, cherry tomatoes and feta cheese, several slices of turkey bacon and a multi-grain bagel, Nate headed to Divine Grace. Once there, he planned to ask his secretary to set up a conference call with King and Derrick, two of his mentors, and see what advice these seasoned men of God could offer in handling a delicate situation such as this.

The early dawn prayer, workout, hot shower and good breakfast had all worked to help calm Nate's angst. But he was still troubled. He tapped the steering wheel, brought up the music library menu and clicked on one of his favorite customized albums. It featured gospel instrumentals from some of his favorites: Kirk Whalum, Paul Jackson, Jr., Ben Tankard, and Johnathan Butler. The first notes of Tankard's version of *Every Praise* had just begun to fill his sedan when the song was interrupted by a phone call. He tapped the telephone icon on the steering wheel.

"Good morning, Ben."

"Nate." His tone implied there was nothing good about this morning. "We've got a situation."

All of the tension removed by the morning's routine came rushing back. *Did something happen to Janet?* If so, he'd never be able to forgive himself.

"Talk to me."

"It's about last Sunday's offering, the one collected at the anniversary program. There's money missing."

Nate exhaled. Thank you, Jesus. Who thought he'd see the day when missing money would leave him feeling relieved and thanking the Lord? Better some missing money, he mused, than a missing church member.

"What happened?"

"Well, he didn't say missing exactly but something's wrong with the deposit. Apparently someone from the bank called the church yesterday looking for Ron, following up on a call they made on Monday afternoon. They said it was urgent. Pam couldn't reach him and called me. I don't know why, but I got a funny feeling about it so instead of passing the message to Ron, I returned the call myself. That's when I realized we might have a problem."

"What did they tell you?"

"That the actual amount deposited didn't equal the amount on the slip. Well, that's not quite right. There was a check in the deposit that looked suspicious. The bank clerk investigated and found that it was linked to an account for a Mrs. Juanita Strong."

"Is she a member?"

"She might have been."

"Was their insufficient funds on the check?"

"Oh, no. The check cleared just fine."

"Then Ben," Nate said, his patience thinning, "I don't understand the problem."

"The problem is the bank clerk just happens to have known Mrs. Strong, a woman who's been dead for almost three years."

"Okay. Now that's a problem."

"Yes, and there's more. This officer knew that Mrs. Strong had quite a bit of money at the time she died and that because her only child had preceded her in death, a nephew in Connecticut had been named executor of her estate. When asked, the nephew said he'd occasionally seen checks made out to the church but since she'd been a staunch supporter of the ministry, he figured it was something she'd set up before she died."

"Maybe she did."

"Somebody did, and that's where it gets interesting. The bank officer did some more digging and finally found out the other authorized name on the account. Are you ready?"

Nate exited the 215 Freeway as a thought hit him like a lightning bolt. "Ron Miller."

"Bingo."

"We both know his moral ineptitude, but how is Ron's name on someone's bank account worthy of a telephone call?"

"The loan officer tracked several of these checks. On or near the same time a check was written on this account, the same or nearly the same amount was deposited into another one."

"An account that belonged to Ronald?"

"He's not that stupid. The money went into the account of an organization called The Rutherford House. I've searched church records back twenty years and find no mention of that name anywhere. But I am ninety-nine point nine percent sure that if we start digging into The Rutherford House, we'll find a connection to Ron."

"Ben," Nate began with a smile in his voice, "if what you say is true this is nothing but God."

"God? Helping Ron steal?"

"No, answering my prayer. I'm almost at the church. Is he there?"

"I haven't seen him."

"Find him. Set up a meeting with him for eleven o'clock. Call a twelve-thirty emergency meeting with the executive branch and deacon board, those who aren't working and can meet. This bank officer, do you have his or her number?"

"The office number and cell number, too."

"Perfect. Get in touch with him and request a meeting as soon as possible. Right now wouldn't be too soon. We're going to open a formal investigation to get to the bottom of this. Ron Miller will be suspended from all executive duties until the matter is resolved in his favor. If he's found guilty, we'll press charges and if I have my way, he'll end up in jail. Where he belongs."

An hour later Nate, Ben and a sleepy-eyed bank

officer named Todd occupied a corner booth at a local diner. The waitress had just seated them and given them menus.

"Anybody need coffee while you decide what you're having?"

"I do," Todd said. "Lots of it."

"Cream and sugar, sir?"

"Black. Strong."

Ben looked at Nate, nodded his head in Todd's direction. "He likes his coffee like I like my women. Todd, you've got good taste."

Nate laughed as Todd's face became almost as red as his hair. "Women? Did you think…I mean, no, I like my…"

By now both Nate and Ben were laughing.

"Relax," Nate said. "It's a cultural expression. He's just teasing."

"Hey, I'm Irish, what do I know?"

"You knew that something was off with that deposit last Sunday, which makes you one fine Irishman in my book."

Ben nodded his agreement. "Anything new since we spoke yesterday?"

Todd pulled out his phone, tapping and scrolling until he found the screen he wanted. "The account was set up in 2011 with signature cards for Mrs. Juanita Strong and Mr. Ronald Miller. Mrs. Strong passed in November of 2012. Checks began clearing on the account in January of 2013."

"For two, almost three years?" Ben exclaimed. "How many checks were there?"

"I didn't record the number of checks in these notes, but I do have the total amount of the checks that were written—$73,026.18."

"Good God!" Ben shouted, causing a couple patrons to look around.

Nate was so shocked he couldn't say anything.

"Did you say seventy thousand, or seven thousand," Ben asked, sure he'd misunderstood.

"Seventy," Todd repeated.

Ben shook his head, his face one of disbelief. "How much was in the account to begin with?"

"$100,000.00. As of last night at closing time there was a balance of $26,973.82."

"How much was the check deposited in Sunday's offering?" Nate asked.

"Twenty-five hundred," Ben said.

"Over the past three years it looks like…" Todd once again checked his phone, "just over thirty-one thousand in checks passed through your ministry."

Nate shook his head. "No wonder the church was broke."

"My guess is that money was taken in a way so as not to draw undue attention to what was happening. A few thousand here and there, several to the church but most of them to a company called," Todd scrolled farther down, "The Rutherford House. The memo section reads 'quarterly charitable donation'."

"We have no member with the last name Rutherford that you can think of?" Ben shook his head. Nate looked at Todd. "Who runs the Rutherford House?"

"That's confidential information that I can't disclose," Todd answered. "The best thing to do would be to open a formal investigation. That way you'll have legal access to bank records and other information, and, more importantly, tangible proof should criminal charges need to be filed."

The waitress returned. "You gentlemen ready to

order?"

"You ordering, Reverend?" Ben asked.

"Just some tea, black, if you have it." He winked at Todd, who blushed again.

"Earl Grey okay?"

"Perfect."

"What about for you, sir?"

Ben looked at Nate. "Do we have time?"

"Sure, get yourself something."

"I'll have the number two with orange juice."

"Just the coffee is fine," Todd said.

As the waitress walked away, Nate's brow furled in thought. "I still don't get this," he said. "Why would Ron write a check to the church and take the church's money? Why not just steal the money right from the account? His name is on it, so that would be legal."

"I thought about that," Todd said. "Here's what I figure. Mr. Miller knew that Mrs. Strong's nephew, the estate's executor, would most likely be viewing the bank statements. If several checks came in made out to Mr. Miller, it would raise a red flag and cause Charles, Mrs. Strong's nephew, to get suspicious. Better to write the checks to the church she belonged to for all those years, or to a charity, and take the money that way. Her penchant for giving to both was well known. When I get to the office, I'll call her nephew and apprise him of the situation. Until this matter is settled, we'll put a hold on the account."

Ben accepted his orange juice from the waitress. "How did this go on for so long without being caught?"

"It's just a fluke that I caught it. Since being promoted, I rarely work with deposits. It just so happened that I covered a buddy's lunch break and was processing deposits, Divine Grace's among them. The only reason the check stood out is because I personally knew Mrs. Strong. Otherwise, the check clears and life goes on, no problem."

"Wow," Nate said, shaking his head in disbelief. "What a God we serve."

"How do you know Mrs. Strong?" Ben asked.

"She was in the same nursing home as my grandmother," Todd said. "They became really good friends. Two months after Mrs. Strong passed, my grandmother died."

"Sorry for your loss, Todd. God put you in the right place at the right time. And you did the right thing. I want you to know how much we appreciate you bringing this matter to our attention."

Not long afterward, Ben's food arrived.

"Eat up," Nate told him as he reheated his tea. "We're headed into battle, the belly of the beast, and will definitely need strength for the fight."

13

"All right, then. I'll catch y'all tomorrow."

Kelvin Petersen gave his teammates a fist bump and handshake then headed to his car. He was tired but pumped. It was game seven and the Suns had to win. They'd fought back from a one and three deficit. To come this close and not take the win would be more than a shame, so much so that Kelvin determined he wouldn't even think about it. He'd focus solely on winning, visualized nothing but the NBA crown. It was time for the Suns to shine!

He slid into his Maserati GranTurismo, a shiny cobalt gray masterpiece with customized tangerine leather seats to match the team colors, a Rouge Acoustic stereo system to play music that inspired, and a complete television and gaming console because boys liked their toys. He pushed a button. The car came to life with Silento singing about whipping and breaking legs.

"Naw, we can't have none of that right now," Kelvin murmured, scrolling through a library of over ten thousand songs cataloged by genre, artist, year and favorites. He found DeJ Loaf featuring Big Sean, punched it in, and turned it up. "Yeah, that's it!" He shifted down to first gear and tapped the gas pedal.

"Back up off us Clippers! We got this! Back the bump up!"

He bobbed his head to the beat as he navigated the streets. When his uncle gave him a basketball as a teenager signed by Shaq and Kobe, nobody knew that it would lead to this. But from the time he hit his growth spurt at the age of thirteen, playing basketball is all he wanted to do. And since meeting her at sixteen, he knew that Princess was going to be his wife.

He took a quick trip down memory lane, back to the day at his dad's house when he first saw her by the pool. They both tried to act nonchalant, as if neither was interested in the other. She spent most of the time on the phone, he recalled. He mostly joked with his best friend who was there, too. Bottom line, he got those digits, though.

His phone rang. He looked at the dash. His spirits took a dive. *I really don't have time for this.* But this situation wasn't about him. He had to take Fawn's call.

"Yo."

"Yo, my ass! Where's my money?"

"Oh, so you are alive and you do still have my number. I knew you'd call if the money dried up."

"Don't play with me," she yelled. "I don't have time for this bullshit."

"I don't either, Fawn!"

As she continued cursing and screaming, Kelvin felt his blood pressure rising. He took deep, calming breaths, called *ujjayi* in yoga. His anger began to recede. Later, he'd surmise that those yoga classes he sometimes endured just to spend time with Princess were more beneficial than he'd realized.

"Kelvin! I know you hear me!"

"Actually, Fawn," he said, his voice low and

unruffled, "you're screaming so loud I can't hear you at all."

"Where. Is. My. Money?!"

"Where's my son?"

"He's not getting beat, despite you thinking otherwise."

"I never accused you of beating him. I just asked if something was going on."

"Yeah, after you interrogated him. Either you or that wench you call wifey. Do you think I don't know what happens when he's over there with you?"

"I'm not going to argue with you, Fawn. You'll get the money when I see my son."

Kelvin disconnected the call and turned up the stereo. He'd gone through a lot of women during those college years and considered himself lucky to have only one baby mama to deal with. In truth, he'd take a dozen others not to have to mess with Fawn. But he was tired of her antics. It was time to involve the courts if necessary. Slowly, his head began to bob. The song's hook to back up fit more scenarios than basketball.

*

Melody sat in her extravagantly-appointed pristine office, one of three in the back rooms of Prestige, a gentlemen's club. She didn't need one, really. Her boyfriend, Harrison Gates, along with his assistant, the accountant, and Melody's personal assistant did all the administrative work; the competent staff of waiters, dancers, bartenders and bouncers did all the rest. Still, she could be found here on most afternoons and early evenings checking the books, going through files, and doing anything else that made her feel important. Like she was really running things the way it appeared, the way she wanted everybody to believe. Perception was reality, right?

Not that all of her time was wasted. Prestige was a members-only club and to weed out the commoners, the entry fee was steep. Like the rungs on her social-climbing ladder, the clientele was among society's elite—celebrities, athletes, businessmen, foreign dignitaries and trust fund babies. Melody made it her business to know their business, and each one by name. It was good to have friends in high places and if possible, for leverage, a compromising picture or video or two.

Behind her back, she was called "pampered pussy." But Melody knew how hard she'd worked to live a luxurious life. She'd laid down with devils and sold her soul. Used her body to climb to the top, with a variety of men such as this club attracted on every rung.

Five years ago she could barely show her face in Dallas, Texas, or anywhere else for that matter. At least in the church world. She was known across the country simply as "the girl in the video." Couldn't get a job. Had no friends. Tried to make amends with Destiny and explain that what had happened hadn't really been her fault. Of course, she didn't listen. Had the roles been reversed Melody wouldn't have listened, either. Her luck changed when a new NFL draft pick arrived in town. She'd poured all of her womanly skills into what was supposed to be a one-night stand. Moved into his house a month later. All was well until his college sweetheart graduated and moved her ass to town.

One monkey didn't stop the show, though. He set her up in a two-bedroom condo, and they continued to groove for another year and a half. Then the girlfriend got pregnant and Melody got dumped. He canceled the lease on the condo and all of her cards. Alone, broke and basically homeless, she'd jumped at the chance to ride to Vegas with a friend who'd gotten a line cook restaurant job at the Rio. She arrived ready to start her life anew—draped in fancy faux diamonds and designer credit card debt.

That weekend at the Voodoo, the hotel's swanky nightclub fifty stories above drunken gamblers wishing on slot machines, dressed in a cashmere mini and thigh-high boots, she was approached by a woman and asked if she modeled. Melody thought it was a pickup line. Instead, the woman handed her a business card. Two weeks later, her friend the cook decided to move in with a co-worker to save money, which left Melody out on the streets again. She found the card, went to Prestige, and quickly became one of their most popular dancers or "specialists" as they were called in this club. Tips were high, propositions were often. But one had to come with deep pockets and a generous spirit to get a taste of Melody's bootyliciousness. She flirted, fed egos and gave a mean lap dance, but went home alone. Until the night Harrison Gates walked into the club, sat at the bar, and watched her dance. A ten-second size up and she knew this man had what she needed and was "ripe to pluck." She'd grabbed the pole and danced for her life. That night, he took her home. She'd mastered separating men from their money years ago. By the next morning, she had his heart. It was a whole twenty-four hours more before she found out he was the owner of the very club where she danced, fresh from a three-week vacation. Her dancing days were over, except for him. And the new life she'd searched for began.

"Hey, baby."

"Hey, Daddy," she purred as Harrison stuck his

head in the door.

"I'm heading out for a couple hours. Do you need anything?"

"As a matter of fact," she began, rising from the chair in a way that displayed the surgically-enhanced assets he'd purchased. "There is something that I need."

She reached the door, pulled him in by his tie, and closed the door behind them.

"No, baby. Come on now, I've got to go."

"Yes, daddy, I know," she cooed, having pushed him on the desk and now deftly unclasped his belt and undid his zipper. "This one's for the road."

Pulling out his limp member, she put almost a decade's worth of experience to work. In short order, she had him hard, resized and satisfied. Without his dose of Viagra, that was hard for the average woman to do. Melody was above average, and not as dumb as she played. She knew a quick blowjob in the office would make it harder to screw whoever he met. That Harrison had other women wasn't a secret. She'd even been with him a time or two and joined in the fun. They were welcome to smash and try and get cash, but if anybody thought they were going to take the throne and replace her in his home, they'd better think again.

Mission accomplished, she sent Harrison on his way, freshened up in her private bathroom, then sat down and tapped her laptop. She checked her social media accounts, posted a couple selfies and then checked emails. There was a message from her mother stating her concern at hearing from her so rarely, encouraging her to come visit, and ending with a scripture. Melody rolled her eyes and deleted the mail. From the time she could remember, she'd wanted to get out from under the thumb of her sanctimonious, judgmental mother and henpecked dad. Getting shipped off to a private Christian school at the age of sixteen was the best thing that had ever happened to her.

The scripture triggered something, though. The memory of her run-in with Destiny. She pulled up a search engine and typed in Divine Grace. The church website came up immediately. Soon she was looking at a handsome, smiling couple and two adorable kids. Pangs of jealousy, remorse and hurt shot through her stomach before she shut down her emotions. All but one, anger. It was an emotion to which she felt entitled given the way she'd been treated the other day at the mall. Destiny had a right to be angry. Melody would give her that. But sleeping with her man was no reason to be disrespectful. Heck, she and Nate weren't even married at the time. When she fucked him, he was still fair game.

"Nate Thicke, as fine as ever." She read their bio, checked out the other tabs on the website, viewed photos of a recent celebration and noted the address.

"You just might get your wish, Mommy," Melody said, slowly turning her office chair this way and that. "Nate Thicke is an enticing reason for me to visit the house of the Lord."

14

At eleven twenty-eight, Nate's secretary, Mrs. Stevens, announced Ronald's arrival. At the same time, per Nate's request, she texted a security guard to come to the executive offices. This precaution wasn't taken for Nate's safety but rather for Ronald's well-being. The guard's nearby presence might keep the senior pastor out of jail.

Ronald tapped on Nate's office door. "You wanted to see me?"

Nate nodded. "Indeed. Come in. Close the door." Ronald did as requested. "Have a seat."

"What's this about, Doc?" he asked, taking a seat in one of two chairs facing Nate's desk.

"Just a minor discrepancy in last Sunday's offering, something that can probably be cleared up quickly."

Ronald sat back, his expression smug. "Already working on that, Rev. Got a call from the bank on Monday. Told them I'd look into it. It's been busy, but I'll take care of that right away."

I just bet you will. Remaining calm was an effort, given how much money this man had stolen from Mrs. Strong and indirectly from the Lord but Nate forced his body to relax and his tone to be casual. He'd spoken briefly with Derrick Montgomery in Los Angeles, who'd cautioned him to be frugal with his words, and how much he knew. Nate planned to say only enough to justify Ronald getting the hell out of the ministry.

"I wish it were that easy to handle but for some reason the bank is all up in arms about it. I guess one of the checks came from an unauthorized account or something. I don't know how all that financial stuff works. But until it's figured out our account is being monitored and part of our funds are frozen."

Nate added the funds frozen part with a straight face, praying forgiveness for the lie. It was to frame the conversation in a way that seemed to hold Ronald blameless, yet justify what was about to take place.

"Don't worry about it. I'll get the hold removed."

"For someone who supervises the team that collects the offerings, and are therefore ultimately responsible for whatever discrepancies occur, you seem totally unperturbed."

"Like I said, I'm looking into the situation. I work with banks all the time. Stuff happens. Maturity allows for calmness until all the facts are known."

How mature and calm were you while giving Janet two black eyes?

Ronald shrugged, looked at his watch, then met Nate's gaze. A raging fireplace could not have crackled more than the tense atmosphere between these two men, both working overtime to appear relaxed.

"Good. Then what I'll have to do now should be easier than I thought. As a matter of protocol, we're going to have to suspend you from all executive and leadership positions until this matter is resolved."

Ronald remained ice cube calm and cucumber cool. "You're kidding, right?"

"I'm afraid not."

"That is not how matters are handled here. The matter has to go to the executive committee. Any actions of that nature must be affirmed by popular vote."

"That's true in most instances. But not this one. It's a matter of security. I'm overriding the rule."

"You can't do that."

"It's already done. Look, Ron, this isn't personal. It's business. And like you said, it's probably something that will be handled quickly. You could be back in as little as a week or two. But for now, I'm going to need your keys."

Ronald's mask of calm slipped just a bit, evidenced by narrowed eyes and a twitching jaw. "You've been trying to push me out of this church since you got here. My brother is the one who preaches rings around you. Why are you so threatened by me?"

A smile appeared on Nate's face. It didn't reach his eyes. "There may be some who fear you. I can assure you that I am not one of them."

"You young mutha—"

"Watch yourself."

"—come into a church that's been in existence for fifty years thinking you can just upend the status quo and change people's lives. We both know this isn't about any got damn money. It's about your wife, and her misinterpreting friendliness for flirtation."

No, it's about the wife who's married to a thief. "Don't bring Destiny into this. In fact, you'd do well to keep all reference to her out of your mouth."

"See, the thing about Destiny," Ronald began, immediately ignoring Nate's suggestion, "is she's probably never been with a real man. Someone who knows how to treat a woman, how to please and satisfy her in every way. So when somebody like myself comes along, a gentleman treating her like a lady, she gets nervous. Or is it tempted? Then scared of an attraction she might not be able to control, she runs to papa to protect her from herself."

Nate's fists ached to connect with Ronald's jaw. He kept them squeezed together beneath the table. "If things don't work out for you as a contractor, you might take up writing. Because what you just said was a nice piece of fiction. Was that right off the top of your head?"

"Exactly what a boy would say when talking to a man."

"I think that's what really bothers you. That a younger man is your physical, intellectual and spiritual superior, one for which your ego makes it hard to respect."

"Respect? Let me tell you something. Respect is earned, especially from some chump like you. Boy, I'm old enough to be your daddy."

"But I'm not a boy. And you're not my daddy. You're the Divine Grace member who I've just suspended. Now, are you going to turn over your keys voluntarily or will they have to be taken from you?"

Ronald gave a humorless snort as he stood. "I wish you'd try."

Nate stood as well. "It would be easy to do."

Ronald took a step forward. Nate stood his ground.

As if by magic, two security guards appeared.

Ronald turned, saw them, and smiled at Nate. "Yeah, you'd better had called for backup."

"Your keys," Nate said.

Ronald slowly reached into his pocket and pulled out a large ring of keys, all the while staring Nate down. He removed a set on its own ring and threw them on Nate's desk.

"Now get out of my office. And while you're on suspension, consider finding a new church home."

One of the bodyguards stepped forward, a hand on the butt of his gun. "Let's go, Mr. Miller."

"This isn't over," he said to Nate.

"Not yet," Nate said, coming from behind his desk and walking toward Ronald. "But it's about to be."

Nate watched Ronald and the guards until they turned the corner. Then he shut his door and plopped down in his seat. Showing restraint had zapped his strength. A full-on butt kicking would have taken less energy.

He tapped the speaker button on the phone, and called Destiny.

"Hey, baby. What's up?"

"I just suspended Ronald."

"Oh my, God, Nate! Why? I told you—"

"Baby, calm down. It's not what you think. It's a financial matter. A loan officer at our bank believes that Ronald has been stealing from a former member, and passing the checks through the church to avoid suspicion."

"What?"

"Yep. More than seventy-thousand dollars over the past three years."

"You cannot be serious!"

"I'm dead serious." He gave her the short version of the breakfast meeting. "I called an executive committee meeting to share what's going on."

"For what time, baby? I'm over here struggling with this speech for the Sanctity of Sisterhood conference. I promised Lady Viv I'd have some type of outline by the end of the day."

"Don't worry about it, Des. Savannah will be here.

I'll fill you in later. Just wanted to let you know what went down so you could make his wife aware of the situation. Ronald was very angry when he left. If it hadn't been for the security guards we might have gone to blows. So call Janet and warn her. If she wants to leave her house, set her up in a hotel. In fact, you might suggest that she do that and give him time to calm down. I don't want the fight meant for me to be taken out on her."

Nate ended the call as Ben walked in.

"You had me worried for a minute there, brother," he said. "I heard voices rise and thought some bumping and thumping was going to come next!"

"It was hard, but I kept my cool. We've already got a violent deacon. Don't need to have a fighting preacher, too."

They headed for the door. Ben opened it and stepped back to let Nate pass. "You ready for this meeting, boss?"

"I'm prayed up, man, and ready for anything."

15

In Lake Las Vegas, Destiny was worried. She couldn't reach Janet. Knowing Ronald was at the church she'd called the burner phone right away. Had left a text and then a voicemail and still received no return call. She left the spa suite and walked to the second-floor sitting room. The beauty of the pale yellow, silk-covered walls, off-white furniture and expensive art went unnoticed as various reasons of why Janet hadn't answered bounced around Destiny's head. The phone could be off or dead, not charged. Janet could have gone out and left the phone at home. Maybe the phone was on silent and Janet was away from it. Maybe Ronald had found it and thrown it away.

"This is so frustrating," she whined to the walls. "Think, Destiny." With a hand to her forehead, she pondered solutions. *Should I take a chance and call her other cell phone, the one Ronald checks?* "Maybe, and then she can delete the call."

She looked at her watch. Twenty minutes had passed. That's about how far the Millers lived from the church. Decision made, Destiny reached for her phone.

It rang in her hand. "Janet! Thank God you called back. I was just about to call your other cell."

"Sorry, First Lady. I didn't realize this phone was out of juice. I had to let it charge for a little while before I could make a call."

"It's okay, I'm just glad I reached you. Listen, something happened at church today. Ronald was suspended."

Janet gasped. "Suspended? Why? How?"

"I don't know the details, but it involves some type of discrepancy in the deposit from this past Sunday's service. Until it's figured out, the church account is frozen and Ron has been sat down."

"Oh, Lord."

"I'm sorry, Janet. Nate called me as soon as their meeting was over. Ronald was angry and Nate, both of us, are concerned about your welfare."

"Oh, Jesus. He's been under so much pressure, lately. This is going to make him very upset."

"Janet, if you want we can put you up in a hotel, no problem. You can stay there until Ron calms down or you figure out what best to do."

"I can't go to a hotel. Ronald would have a fit if he came home and didn't find me here!"

"He might have a fit either way! Wouldn't you rather experience it from a distance, say over a cell phone?"

"You don't how Ronald is, Lady. He doesn't like me doing things that weren't discussed with him beforehand." Destiny could hear what sounded like pacing or items being moved around, noise in the background.

"Janet, what are you doing?"

"I'm looking to see if we have steaks in the freezer. Ronald loves my steaks. Maybe his favorite meal will calm him down."

Destiny bit back a response. She'd never been in

Janet's shoes, and didn't have the right to try and tell her how to walk in them. "What about Roy's wife, your sister-in-law. Can she help you somehow, maybe come over or let you go to her?"

"Bethany works. And even if she was home, I wouldn't bother her. She's tried to get me to leave Ronald for years and when I wouldn't she told me to stop talking to her about it. That if I got beat up again she didn't want to know."

"Janet, I know you love your husband but you can't keep living like this!"

"I don't want to, but it's how I've lived since I was seventeen years old."

"All the more reason to not suffer more abuse. You're not alone, Janet. Nate and I are here to help you. There are services and programs available to provide information and a network of resources. If you get a restraining order—"

"Ha! Like he'd pay any attention to that. Lady, I appreciate you calling, but I need to go."

"Okay, Janet, but stay in touch with me. If you can't call, send a text so that I know you're all right."

"Will do."

"If I don't hear from you they'll be someone at your door. Got it?"

"Yes, Lady. I'll call you. But I'll be fine."

Destiny hung up the phone and prayed those words were true.

*

Back at Divine Grace, the seven board members available on short notice had gathered in the boardroom along with Nate, Ben and Savannah, Nate's secretary, Mrs. Stevens, Roy Miller, an associate minister, and Ed Bailey, a deacon and one of the oldest members of the church.

"Good afternoon, everyone," Nate began. "First of all I want to thank all of you for breaking away from your normal routine to attend this emergency board meeting. I'm sure you're all wondering what this is about, and I won't drag out this meeting or hold you in suspense for too much longer."

"Excuse me, Reverend," Roy said, a slight scowl marring his smooth brown skin. "I'm sorry to interrupt, but shouldn't Ron be here? If you didn't get him at the office, I'm almost sure he'll answer his cell."

"Thank you, Reverend Miller. I've already spoken to your brother so he's well aware of everything that will be discussed here today." Nate paused, and glanced around the room for signs of more questions. Seeing none, he continued.

"On Monday, the office received a call about last Sunday's offering, the monies raised during the anniversary program. It appears that something wasn't quite right with the deposit. There was a discrepancy in what was on the deposit slip versus the actual monies turned in."

"A discrepancy as in money missing?" one board member asked.

"Something like that," Nate responded. "Before I go further let me say this. We don't yet have all of the facts surrounding this situation but it is one that has caused one of the bank's officers enough concern to warrant a thorough investigation. Until the matter is resolved, we're going to limit access to church funds and keep a very close record of what is deposited and withdrawn."

"I still don't understand why my brother isn't here," Roy mumbled.

"Reverend Miller, that brings me to my next point.

Ronald Miller, the finance director as all of you know, has been suspended pending the resolution of this situation."

Various mumblings broke out amid the members.

"Oh my goodness!"

"Did I hear that right?"

"Suspended?"

Nate remained quiet, letting the expected outcry die down on its own.

"Why would he be suspended?" Roy asked. "Seems like since this is a financial situation, he's the main one who should be here."

"Some cookies are missing," Ed Bailey offered, his slow, country drawl dragging out each word. "They obviously think his hand might have been in the jar."

"That's preposterous!" The usually placid Reverend Miller got more riled up by the second. "You think my brother stole money? That's nonsense."

"No one has been accused or absolved," Nate calmly responded. "But due to the nature of the discrepancy and, as the person in charge of and responsible for deposits, Deacon Miller was suspended as a matter of protocol."

"Protocol?" This suspicion-laced word came from Donetta Logan, an attractive woman in her sixties who'd retired from Boeing with a nice pension that she'd increased by flipping houses. It had long been rumored that she and Ronald had once been an item. Whether or not this was true had never been confirmed. "The protocol for any action involving suspending or firing anybody is that it be put before the board for a vote. That's the protocol at Divine Grace."

"You are correct, Ms. Logan. Unless the senior pastor feels the need to override that article due to either the security or safety of this building and/or its members."

"Ain't this nothing," Roy spat out as he squirmed in his chair. "Man, you're acting like my brother's a criminal or something. Talking about security and safety like Ron's going to come in here and shoot up the place."

"I understand your outrage, Roy, and your displeasure at what's happening. Ronald wasn't happy either and, quite frankly, neither am I. This situation puts all of us in an awkward position and the finances of the church in jeopardy. As I told Ronald, this isn't personal, it's business. I did what I felt led to do, and take full responsibility for my actions and any consequences that result from them."

The associate minister spoke up. "How long is this investigation supposed to take?"

"They're working on it right now and have already made quite a bit of progress. But something as sensitive as this can't be rushed or handled too quickly. They didn't give me a timeframe, but I'd hope no more than a couple weeks."

"Who is this bank officer?" Donetta asked. "And who besides you knows what's going on?"

"Brother Ben and his wife, Savannah, are fully apprised of the situation, as is an outside investigation team."

Donetta crossed her arms across an ample bosom. "I think as members of the executive board we all have a right to know the details."

"And you will, Ms. Logan, but due to the sensitive nature of this situation, Brother Ben and I are proceeding as we've been advised."

"So Ronald's been suspended as finance director. But he's still head deacon, right?"

"No, Roy. Ronald has been relieved from all executive and leadership responsibilities pending the outcome of this matter."

Murmuring began again, louder this time.

"Now, Reverend, I have to stop you there," the associate minister said as he got to his feet. "When it comes to the deacons and trustees of this church, you can't just arbitrarily remove them from an elected position. Ron's been the head deacon at this church for what, ten or fifteen years? You don't have the authority to sit him down like that."

Rather than respond to the minister directly, Nate addressed the group. "I knew the responses to this decision would be varied, and I understand those of you who are upset, especially those of you who are long-time members. I wouldn't want any of you to be where you're unhappy."

"Are you suggesting we leave the church?" Roy asked, now joining the associate minister who was still on his feet. "You're the one who just got here, Reverend. As you just stated, all of us have been here for a very long time. So, if things aren't going well and somebody needs to leave, seems to me that ought to be you."

"Him leave?" Deacon Ed looked at Roy as though a horn had sprouted in the middle of his forehead. "Reverend Thicke is the only reason these church doors are still open. Before he arrived this church couldn't pay attention, much less a light bill. Instead of getting all hot and bothered, we ought to be supporting this investigation or whatever they're doing. Maybe it will help us understand why there's been so little money for the last four or five years."

He looked at Nate. "You do what you need to do, Reverend Thicke. There are more for you than against you, and we'll all be praying this thing right on through."

"I appreciate that, Deacon Ed. We all need to pray. In fact, that's how we'll close this meeting. With a word of prayer. Would everyone stand?" Nate stood, along with the others. "Deacon Ed, will you lead us to the throne of grace?"

Everyone bowed their head and closed their eyes. Except for Nate, who trusted God but didn't trust man. He prayed with one eye open.

16

Melody entered Prestige and looked around. It was not yet three p.m. yet the room held a fair number of clients. This was an expectation rather than a surprise. The club had always been popular. When Harrison bought it, he took it up several notches. He remodeled and expanded the interior with plush carpeting, slick marble, ebony wood, crystal chandeliers and a state-of-the-art kitchen for their Michelin-starred chef. Beautiful, highly educated, sexually fluid women, called specialists, replaced the cute but average dancers who'd once adorned the poles. It became a private club with a steep membership fee and an application that included an extensive background check. Nothing made a place hotter than making it difficult to get inside. There were three levels of membership. A VIP clearance cost a cool twenty-five thousand, with acceptance solely at Harrison's discretion. This fee included top shelf drinks and other mind-altering substances if requested, car service, complimentary meals, special seating, and special access to the specialists. Many had paid it without batting an eye. Others hadn't, but wished they could.

She nodded and waved at a few friendly faces as

she walked to the bar and took a seat. Directly in her line of vision on the other side of the long, gleaming counter was a well-dressed man she didn't recognize. He had a close-cropped haircut and a salt-and-pepper goatee. His suit was tailored and his cuff links were gold. He looked like someone she ought to know. She moved to the other side.

The bartender came right over. "Good afternoon, Ms. Anderson. The usual?"

"Yes, please."

"One glass of Grand Cuvee Brut coming right up."

"Thank you, darling."

Melody set down her oversized designer bag and pulled out her phone. The businessman to her left spoke immediately, complimenting her choice of perfume. But the stranger to her right never looked up, just stared at the tumbler of brown liquor in front of him. He slowly reached for the glass, drained it, and signaled the bartender for a refill.

His inattentiveness further got Melody's attention. With a subtle nod to the bartender, she transferred the stranger's bar tab to her own. Ten minutes later, he motioned the bartender over to settle up.

"No balance, sir. You're good to go."

"What do you mean?"

"Your tab's been paid, sir."

"By whom?"

The bartender looked at Melody. The stranger followed his eyes. Melody smiled. The stranger walked over. "You paid my bill?"

"I did."

"Why?"

"It looked like you could use a kind gesture."

"I looked that bad?"

"Worse."

The stranger smiled and extended his hand. "Ron Miller."

"Melody."

"No last name?"

"None needed for casual encounters."

"It'll be casual, all right. I'm not about to go to jail for being with a minor. Are you sure you're allowed in here?"

"Legal enough, our conversation won't send you to jail."

Ron sat down. "You work here?"

"You could say that."

"I don't remember seeing you dance so…you're an assistant?"

"I'm the owner."

Ronald's brow raised as he looked her up and down. Melody's hair and nails were flawless, the haute couture dress hugged T&A just right, stilettos emphasized her curvy calves and elongated her legs, and real diamonds dripped off of her ears and wrists. Melody knew she oozed affluence and that the stranger had taken notice. As he should.

"The owner, huh? Either that's true or you have one heck of a sugar daddy taking care of you."

Melody placed a soft hand on his arm now resting on the counter. "Trust me, I can take care of myself." She waited until the bartender had taken her glass and walked away, then turned to Ronald again. "What has a handsome man like you drowning his sorrows in the middle of the day?"

"What makes you think I'm sorrowful?"

"Careful observation."

"So you've been checking me out?"

"An impressive-looking man like you is hard to miss."

That this comment pleased Ron showed on his face. He looked down at her hand. "That's a beautiful ring."

"Thank you."

"Unusual for a wedding ring, but very nice."

"I'm not married. However," she hurried on before he could speak, "I'm not available either. Just," she paused, bit her lip, and twirled her shoulder-length tresses, "a shameless flirt."

"Baby girl, flirting while looking and smelling all good the way you do can get you in a whole lot of trouble."

"If it did, you look like the type of man who could get me out."

"I'm scared of you!"

They laughed. The bartender brought both Ronald and Melody fresh drinks. They toasted. "Now, what happened today to cause the frown I saw when I first arrived?"

That smile, soft voice and innocent demeanor had coaxed secrets out of more men than Melody could count on fingers and toes. From the time she'd lost her virginity, Melody had used sex as a tool to get ahead in life. Whatever one may feel about women who used their bodies this way, the plan had served her well.

"Just a little problem with business, that's all. Nothing that can't be handled."

"What kind of business?"

"I'm a building contractor. My company specializes in unique construction types. We also put in special security for some of the wealthier residents. Earthquake bunkers, safe rooms, escape tunnels…stuff like that."

"Sounds exciting."

"It can be."

"Do you have a card?"

"Sure." He pulled one out and gave it to her.

Melody's phone vibrated. She looked at its face, then placed it and Ronald's card in her bag and stood. "Mr. Miller, I have to run. It was a pleasure speaking with you."

She held out her hand, which he raised to his lips.

"I can assure you, the pleasure was all mine."

"You came in disgruntled, but I want you to leave happy so food, drink, women…it's all on the house. My treat."

"That's very generous. Thank you, Ms. Melody with no last name."

She winked and was gone. Two seconds into the hallway, and Ron Miller's name had been typed into the search engine. By the time she reached her plush, corner office, she knew his full name. Five minutes later, she'd logged into her background check account and had his recent work history, the name of his wife, immediate family and a tidbit that interested her more than all of the others put together. His affiliation with Divine Grace Community Center, her ex-friend Destiny's church.

"Ronald F. Miller," she purred, looking at the business card he'd given her. "A member of my old lover's church and a way for me to get information. I might have to plan a shopping spree so you and I can spend some quality time together."

She didn't stray often but every now and then, when Melody needed something long, hard, thick and young, she planned a shopping trip to LA. "Me time," is how she explained it to Harrison. He never questioned her. She imagined that while gone he was equally busy. Her man was intelligent and astute, but had no street smarts.

Melody knew that he was paying the bouncer five-hundred a week to keep an eye on her. What Harrison didn't know is that Melody was paying that same bouncer seventy-five hundred every seven days to see only what she wanted her husband to know.

For now, she had nothing to hide. But to get the kind of information on Destiny from Ronald Miller that might prove useful, she might have to keep a secret or two.

17

Both were mentally exhausted and tempted to cancel but that night, at seven-thirty, Nate and Destiny boarded a private plane headed for Phoenix, courtesy of Princess Brook Petersen. The game would have started by the time they got there, but considering the tsunami of drama they'd survived the past twenty-four hours it was a miracle that they were showing up at all. Having powered through the day on an hour's sleep, Nate's head was rolling before the plane left the runway. Unfortunate for Destiny, since she'd planned to use Nate's input to tweak the outline for her Sanctity of Sisterhood speaking engagement. She pulled out her iPad and fired it up. Reading what she had so far felt appropriate but uninspired.

With the organization's name as a guide she'd tentatively titled her talk *Sister To Sister,* and thought to focus on how differently women acted in the 21st century as compared to twenty, fifty or a hundred years ago. The b-word, for example, which at one time could get a fight started, was now a term of endearment. How did that happen, and were we as a collective sisterhood better off in a society that embraced the word? This topic was listed under the bullet point, respect. Other bullet points were loyalty, friendship, networking and support. She wanted to encourage women her age to see each other more as friends than enemies. As someone who'd grown up with her share of detractors and few female friends, she didn't want this only for the group she'd address, but for herself as well.

Forty-five minutes later Nate woke up, just as they were landing. Destiny was still not satisfied with the outline, but having promised it to Vivian before the day was over she quickly attached it to an email and pressed send.

She wanted to be angry but one look into the puppy dog eyes of her sleepy husband, and her heart melted. When straightening the collar of his sports jacket, she wasn't able to resist a little blessing out.

"Thanks for helping with my outline, Mr. National Speaker, prolific preacher and bestselling author."

"Sorry, baby," Nate offered amid a yawn. "I'll go over it after the game, promise."

"No worries. I promised Vivian I'd have it to her today so I just sent what I had."

"I'm sure it's amazing." He leaned over and kissed her. "Just like you."

"Yeah, yeah, yeah, tell me anything to get yourself off the hook."

When they reached ground transportation, a town car was waiting. The couple arrived at the VIP entrance of the US Airways Center and were quickly whisked inside where an usher planned to take them to the seat numbers printed on their tickets, just rows from the floor.

"Baby, go ahead and sit with Princess. Derrick sent me a text while we were in the air. I'm going to join the fellas in the suite."

"Okay, babe." She leaned in for a quick kiss on the

lips, and followed the usher into the arena while a guard took Nate down the hall to the elevator and the suites.

Destiny stepped through the arena doors and was immediately assaulted by the roar of the crowd. The score was tight, Suns led by four points. She reached the aisle just as Kelvin outmaneuvered the man guarding him and executed a fade-away jumper. Swish! Nothing but net.

Destiny looked up to see Princess yelling and waving. She wore four-inch heels, but Destiny climbed the stairs like she was in Nikes, and pushed past girlfriends and wives to the empty seat next to Princess.

"Hey, girl!"

"Destiny!"

They shared a heartfelt hug.

"About time you got here." Princess looked toward the stairs. "Did Nate go the suite?"

"Uh-huh."

"What took you guys so long? I called the pilot. He was there for almost an hour before you showed up."

"You didn't get my text?"

"Yes, I did and...hello! Game seven? Conference finals? Clippers and Suns? What church stuff short of Jesus coming back couldn't wait until tomorrow?"

Destiny rolled her eyes and waved her off. "After dealing with it the past twenty-four hours that's the last thing I want to talk about."

Princess's teasing voice turned to one of concern. "But everything's okay?"

"No, girl, stuff's a mess. Let's talk later. Go, Kelvin!"

"Go, baby!" Princess yelled, cupping her mouth with her hands. "Let's go Suns!"

"Did Pastor King make it?" Princess nodded. "And

your mom, too?"

"Yes, but she cares nothing about basketball. She's watching Kiara."

"Kiara and Kelly?"

"No, just Kiara."

Destiny turned from the game to look at Princess. "I thought you told me Kelly would be here this weekend."

"I did."

"What happened?"

"Girl," she began, mocking Destiny. "That's the last thing I want to talk about right now."

The friends laughed and spent the rest of the half cheering on the Suns.

*

Upstairs in the suite the men were totally focused, as if by sheer concentration they could help Kelvin win.

"Aw, man!" Derrick yelled, standing up for emphasis. "That was a foul, ref. Seriously?" He turned to King and Nate. "Did y'all see that?"

"That was just a hand check," King replied. "The kind I use on the court to beat your behind."

Derrick sat down and reached for his soda. "Man, I play better on my worse day than you do on your best."

King looked at Nate. "See, what kind of jaw-jacking I've had to put up with for the last thirty years?"

Nate offered a lazy smile, then reached for the black tea he'd ordered to try and wake up.

King eyed him more closely. "Man, you're looking pretty beat. Does it have anything to do with why you were late tonight?"

Nate yawned, rubbed his hands over his face. "It has everything to do with it." A beat and then, "I had to suspend the deacon."

This statement took Suns diehard Derrick's attention

away from the game. "The one you called us about earlier?"

"Yep. Ronald Miller."

"He admitted to domestic violence." King turned away from the game, too.

"No. He didn't admit to stealing either."

"Wait a minute." King sat back, then leaned forward. "What?"

"Long story short, we believe that Ron was using a check fraud scheme to steal money from the church. It hasn't been proven which is why he's suspended, not fired and barred. As bad as that is, God answered my prayer. I wanted him gone for beating up Janet. But she didn't want him to know that we knew. So God gave me a way to get rid of him and not tip her hand."

Derrick raised a brow. "You dealt with all of that today?"

"Pretty much."

"What about the wife? Is she all right?"

"As far as we know. Just before taking off, Destiny texted her. I don't know whether or not she's heard back."

"How's Destiny doing? You said he'd disrespected her, too."

"She's stressed, worried about Janet. She's one of Destiny's assistants who supported us from day one, and has always been there for my wife. Plus, I don't think Destiny has told me everything where Ron is concerned. He always flirted with her, but he flirts with everybody. Looking at Destiny, you can see why, so I gave him a pass. Several months ago when it got out of hand, we talked about it. He said he understood and that it wouldn't happen again. If I'd known then how badly his actions had affected my wife there wouldn't have been much talking."

"I hear you, man," Derrick said. "Anybody disrespecting Vivian would get the left hook of fellowship right out of my sanctuary."

"Stealing from the Lord!" King shook his head, and reached for one of the baby back ribs on his plate. "That's some lowdown crime."

"He's a lowdown dude."

"How much did he steal?" Derrick asked.

"Allegedly," Nate said, putting the word in air quotes, "enough to put him behind bars and away from his wife. And I say hallelujah to that."

*

After chatting with some of the friendlier wives, Princess and Destiny went to the restroom to freshen up before halftime was over.

"It's nice to see there are actually basketball wives who aren't nasty and catty," Destiny said when they were alone.

"The two I introduced to you are really nice. We've actually gotten together as families, our children play together, stuff like that." Princess pulled out a tube of lipstick and touched up her lips. "But don't let your guard down, because some of the women…" She finished the sentence with a shake of her head.

"Sounds like they could use the speech I'm going to give at next month's SOS meeting." Destiny eyed herself in the mirror, and wearing almost no makeup just fluffed up her hair.

"You wrote it?"

"Don't I wish. I've struggled forever just to get through an outline."

"You're probably being hard on yourself. I'm sure

it's fine."

"We'll see." Destiny leaned on a counter as she faced Princess. "Now, tell me what's going on with Kelly and whatshername."

"Girl," Princess gave a sound of disgust. "I'm so done with her. She's refusing to let Kelly come here because Kelvin called her, concerned about their son's behavior."

"What, he was acting out?"

"Just the opposite. Kelly has always been fun, outgoing. But the last couple visits, he's been quieter than usual. Honestly, Kelvin noticed it more than I did, but they spend more time together. When Kelvin called Fawn with his concern she tripped, as per usual, and didn't return Kelvin's phone call until today. And that's only because he held up her check. He told her no son, no money." Princess shut her compact as an exclamation point. "The ball's in her court. We'll see how it bounces."

"It's so weird that she'd keep him from Kelvin. He's been coming down here for what, the last three or four years?"

"She moved a new boyfriend into her house. I think little man is just mad about his king of the castle demotion. And I think Fawn uses every opportunity to get Kelvin's attention, even if it's negative. Ooh! That's the buzzer. Let's get back to the game."

Not long after returning to her seat, Kelvin glanced over. Princess blew him a kiss and gave a thumbs up. For the next hour, the two teams battled it out. The lead changed hands over and again. The Suns got in foul trouble and had to sit out their star forward. Kelvin helped to pick up the slack but with two minutes remaining, the Clippers led by six points. Kelvin got fouled and made one of two shots. The Suns put on a full-court press. Their cagey point guard stole the ball for two. It was a battle of warriors but when the buzzer sounded, one point cost Kelvin's team the chance to play for the NBA championship. Unfortunately, the game of life would mirror the game at the arena. There would be more losers.

18

Late the following morning at the quiet Petersen mansion, a sumptuous brunch was being prepared. Princess didn't employ a full-time chef but had one on-call for special occasions and days like this, when they had guests. Today's menu included a smoothie and fresh fruit bar for the health-conscious, German chocolate waffles and butter pecan pancakes for those not calorie-counting, various types of bacon and sausage including a vegan option, eggs to order and drinks of choice. Princess and the chef had planned a menu that would suit every palate. More than a dozen family and friends were scattered throughout the house, minus Destiny and Nate, who had business back in Nevada. This was meant to be a time of celebration but with the Sun's nail-biting loss, the brunch would be a subdued if not downright somber affair. Not to mention Destiny's erroneous assumption that Princess thought Kelly was being sexually abused. Princess knew assaults happened against children, but surely Fawn would be aware of something that egregious. The thought was unfathomable, but it lingered.

Princess finished consulting with the chef, checked on Kiara, then headed for the other side of the house and

Tai's guest suite. She knew her father was already up and out. He'd left before eight for a round of golf with Derrick, who'd also spent the night. If Kelvin's uncle and cousins were up, they were likely poolside. Same for Princess's brother, Michael, who was in town with a date. Given that their parents were there she'd given the two love birds separate rooms. But knowing her brother and the cute sister with short, curly locs and the kind of natural booty that celebrities paid for, they hadn't spent the entire night alone.

Princess reached the double doors to Tai's suite and gave a light knock. Not hearing an answer, she eased open the door to the sounds of new age music, an instructor's soft recorded voice, and her mother facing downward dog on a mat.

"I didn't know you were doing yoga. You should have called me so I could join you."

"I just started."

"Oh." Then on second thought, "never mind."

"Ha!" Tai listened for the next instruction and continued the routine.

"You do this every morning?"

"I try. Stretching helps me gather and focus my thoughts. Plus, it's a calming way to begin the day. You ought to try it."

"Mom, I've been doing yoga regularly for over a year. I thought you knew."

"It may have slipped my mind."

"Given that trying it out as a stress reliever was your suggestion, I'd say that's a good possibility. I'll join you tomorrow."

"Okay." Tai went from a twisting triangle to a side plank. "How's Kelvin?"

"As well as can be expected, I guess."

"You guess?"

"He didn't sleep in our room last night. After that kind of loss he needs little conversation and lots of alone time. I know he blames himself."

"Why?"

"For not being one-hundred percent focused, and for missing a free throw at the end of the game. We lost by one point, which of course he thinks was his missed second free throw. I've learned that there is no convincing him when he's like that. So I listen, and try to be as supportive as I can."

"He's concerned for the welfare of his child. I'm sure that under the circumstances he did the best that he could."

"He did better than that. At not even one-hundred percent he still had the second-highest score and third-highest number of rebounds. He played his heart out and left it all on the court. Now isn't the time to tell him that. I know he and Uncle Derrick talked for a long time last night. Knowing Uncle, Kelvin was left with a different perspective than one he would have reached on his own."

"I'm sure. Is he still here?"

Princess nodded. "He and Daddy are on the golf course." She looked at her watch. "They should be getting back soon. I told them brunch was at eleven. And you can't hide from daddy by eating in your room."

"Child, I told you I was teasing the other day. Nobody's hiding from King."

"I sure hope not, considering you guys have known each other since you were in diapers."

That was practically true. Derrick, King and Tai had all grown up in Kansas City, and spent almost all of their school years together. At fourteen, Tai met Vivian on a trip to the National Baptist Convention and later invited her to a revival she attended with King. The guest speaker was Derrick Montgomery. Vivian saw him. Derrick saw her. And here, twenty-five years later, they were not only friends but practically family.

All things considered, brunch was a lovely affair. King and Tai chatted amicably, catching up Princess on her grandparents, the good Reverend Doctor and Mama Max Brook, her twin siblings back in Kansas and the extended family. She was glad for the chatter. It kept her from having to lead the conversation. Her thoughts were on Kelvin and how long the harrowing, one-point loss to the Clippers would torment him.

*

Upstairs in his man cave, Kelvin was indeed tormented. But last night's game wasn't on his mind. He was thinking about Kelly, and the feeling he couldn't shake that something was going on with his child. What Princess said was true. Fawn had used her pregnancy with Kelly to try and trap him, and continued to use the child as a reason to stay in their lives. But that didn't explain his son's behavior the last couple of times he'd stayed at their home. How could Fawn have influenced his somber mood and reluctance to talk? Princess wouldn't put anything past his ex, including manipulating Kelly for selfish gain. He wouldn't either. But what could she have done, told the boy to act as if something was wrong when it wasn't? Ordered him to shut down like a mute if Kelvin asked a question? Under normal circumstances, he would trust Princess's intuition. In this instance, he felt her acrimonious history with Fawn was interfering with her ability to accurately judge her hunches. How else could he explain Princess's belief that Fawn's actions were the same old trickery while everything in his gut felt that something more was wrong?

Kelvin reached over and grabbed his phone off the nightstand.

"Kelvin. What's up buddy?"

"Hey, Brandon."

"Tough loss last night. I was feeling for you out there."

"Yeah, losing by one point is crushing, especially when it's the one I missed at the free throw line."

"I knew you'd think of it that way, instead of remembering that it took four quarters and five guys on the court every minute of the game and every game of the tournament. You played hard, Kelvin. I hope in time you can see that the loss wasn't your fault, or anybody's for that matter. You're both solid, good teams. Last night could have gone either way and it went theirs. Sorry, man."

"I appreciate it."

"I was surprised to see your name on my screen. After some of those UCLA losses, we wouldn't see you for days."

"I'm shocked, too, but life has a way of putting things in perspective. Like realizing that there are worse things that can happen besides losing a game, even one as important as a division championship." He paused, realizing in that moment that his maturity had gone to another level. "I'm worried about Kelly."

"Fawn's kid? What happened?"

Kelvin told him. "I couldn't even be a hundred percent on the court. At any given moment at least one or two percent of my thoughts were on him and the reason she canceled his last two visits and stopped taking my calls."

"Man...that sounds like Fawn's usual drama. You know how she is."

"I know how Kelly is, too. And he's not that quiet, shy kid who came here last month."

"What does Princess think?"

"Same as you, that Fawn's being messy and nothing is really wrong. I would prefer that to tell you the truth. She started dating somebody a few months ago and just moved him into the house. Nobody knows the dude. I think that's what is making me so uncomfortable. I don't care that Fawn is seeing somebody. In fact, I'm glad that somebody is taking her attention off of me. I just want to know who it is and have a chance to meet him. I need to feel cool about who Fawn has in the house, who's living with my son. The only other contact I have to her is a cousin who swears she doesn't know as much as me."

"I lost contact with the old crew too, but there are a couple people I can call who might have some info. Let me do that and hit you back."

"I appreciate that, Bran."

"I've got your back at all times. You know that."

They ended the call, and Kelvin lay back against the bed. His heart felt lighter, much to his surprise. It wasn't that he didn't hurt over losing to the Clippers. Knowing the Suns were the better team and should have won made it hurt like hell! But doing something about Kelly's situation eased the tightness in his gut. He couldn't change the game score. That was in the past. Focusing on something he could do felt much more productive.

Kelvin got up and took a long, hot shower. He dressed, and when he went back to his phone saw that he'd missed a call from Brandon. He tapped redial.

"That was quick," he said, when Brandon answered.

"Hey, I lucked out. Called one of my boys who was over to a friend's house and he knew Fawn and this guy."

"Who's the friend?"

"I don't even know. Didn't think to ask. He just gave me a name—Gerald Packard."

Kelvin tapped the speaker icon so that he could talk and search at the same time. "You say, Packard? P-a-c-k…"

"A-r-d. First name, Gerald."

"What the hell?"

As he read the first headline, his heart raced.

Burnsville man charged after saying he sexually abused…

"What is it?"

"Hold up." He clicked on the link to the entire article. "Oh, okay. I saw a headline about a sexual abuser. But this guy lives in Minnesota and is seventy years old."

"That ain't him."

"I'll keep searching. Thanks for your help, Brandon. When I find something, I'll let you know."

An hour later, Kelvin went looking for Princess. He found her in the TV room, watching a Disney movie with Kiara and Tai.

She looked up, surprised. "Kelvin! I'm surprised to see you."

"I know, right? I need to talk to you."

"Sure." She followed him out of the room. "What is it, baby? You look so serious."

"I found out the name of the dude living with Fawn, put it in the search engine and don't like what came up."

"Who is he?"

"His name is Gerald Packard. And he's someone I don't want anywhere around my son."

"Why? What did he do?"

"I'll tell you on the way to LA. I already called the pilot. He's gassing up the plane."

"What? You're going to LA right now? Kelvin, what did you read about this guy where this trip can't wait until Monday?"

"Look, if you don't want to go, stay here. But I'm going to LA to see about my child."

19

In Lake Las Vegas, Destiny held the phone listening to her mother sing.

"You feel like your whole world is under attack,
For every step forward there are ten steps back.
But God sent me to tell you. Hang on.
The darkest part of night is just before dawn.

"Da, da, da da..." Simone stopped singing. "I need another line for this verse."

"Mom, I can so relate to the words you've written so far. I think a lot of people can."

"Mark loves it, too. In fact, he's encouraging me to record it and put it on Youtube, or one of those independent music sites."

"That's a great idea! It could go viral and who knows what might happen. You could get a record deal!" Destiny's phone beeped. "Oh, Mom, I have to take this call. It's Lady Viv."

"All right sweetie. We'll talk soon."

Destiny clicked over. "Good afternoon, Lady."

"And a good afternoon Lady yourself."

Destiny chuckled. "It's still so weird to hear myself referred to like that."

"It's what you envisioned, what you prayed for."

"I prayed to be Nate's wife. All this other stuff is extra."

The sister-girl tone she adopted while saying this made Vivian laugh. "Yes, being a preacher's wife can be too much extra at times. But whatever God brings us to, he'll take us through."

"Amen. I got your reply that you received my outline. Have you read it?"

"I did."

"What do you think?"

"I think we've got something to work with."

"Hmm, that doesn't sound too good."

"Better something to work with than nothing at all. I like the overall concept. It embraces exactly what SOS stands for, what we're about. What we need to do to take this to the next level is to establish a personal connection between you and some of these topics, which will in turn establish a rapport with the audience and make each point that much more relatable to them."

"What do you mean?"

"Take, for instance, loyalty. Your life was turned upside down because you were betrayed. Now, you don't have to put all your business out there—"

"Too late! Already done!"

Vivian laughed. "I wasn't going to go there. But speaking in general terms, you can share how betrayal made you feel and how God helped you get through it. Personal examples, a personal perspective, is what will connect you with your audience, and the women in the audience to you."

"You make it sound easy. I've never given a speech in my life."

"It's just talking, that's all. Like you and I are talking right now. And putting that conversation on paper."

Destiny sighed. "Are you sure you can't get Princess to do it again? The women attending won't mind. They love her!"

"They'll love you, too. Have faith and remember I'm always here, Destiny, and any of the other first ladies who've done this. Carla is an excellent resource. Do you have her number?"

"Yes, I do."

"Give her a call. She'll give you some great tips."

"Okay."

"How is life otherwise?"

"This week was a horror show."

"Oh, my. That's a ghastly description, no pun intended. What happened?"

"Remember the Miller brothers, the ones we talked about at dinner last Sunday?"

"Yes."

"The head deacon, Ronald, beat up his wife. On top of that he's suspected of stealing money from the church and got suspended."

"Wow. All of that happened this week?"

"All of that happened since Wednesday."

"Good Lord, Destiny. How is the woman?"

"Her name is Janet. Please lift her up in prayer."

"I certainly will."

"As for how she's doing, she's frightened but trying to be strong. Nate said Ron was livid when he left the church. I called Janet and warned her. True to form, he came home late last night and started in on her—arguing, threatening. She knew what was next. I'd arranged a hotel room should she need it. When he went into the bathroom, she left."

"She's at the hotel now?"

"Yes. I talked with her earlier and suggested she stay

at least until tomorrow, and to ignore Ron's calls. She needs time to think on her own. Without his influence."

"Very good advice, First Lady."

"I have a pretty good mentor," Destiny said with a smile.

"Do you think she's going to follow it?"

"I do. She's been abused for a very long time. But I think she's ready for change."

*

Janet sat on the bed, looking at her phone as it rang yet again. Since leaving the house at midnight, Ronald had called and texted nonstop. She was as afraid to answer the phone as she was to leave it alone. But Lady Destiny had asked her not talk to Ronald and she said she'd try. So she was trying.

The ringing stopped. She picked up the phone. There were twelve messages. Against her better judgment, she tapped the voicemail icon.

The automated voice seemed louder than usual. *You have twelve new messages. First new message.*

"Where the hell are you?"

Ronald's voice boomed from the speaker. Janet swore the room got dark. Her thumb trembled. Delete.

New message.

"You left the house? In my car? Have you lost your mind? Get back here. Now!"

Her thumb hovered over the word. Delete.

New message.

"Janet, I'm not playing with you. If you're not in this house in the next ten minutes, it's going to be a problem."

She turned away as if the message itself could see her, closed her eyes and tapped the screen. Delete.

New Message.

"Dammit Janet. It's been thirty minutes. Nothing you needed could have taken this long. You know this is trouble, right?"

She looked over at the mirror, nodded at her image. To defy Ronald was definitely a troubling thing to do. Delete.

New message.

"You think you can run from me? Is that what this is? I'm going to find you, wherever you're at. You hear me?"

Janet gritted her teeth against the fear of this reality. She looked at the door, stood, walked over and checked the peephole. There was no one there. Looking at the phone, she poised her thumb over the delete button, stopped, and tapped save instead.

New message.

"Janet, I'm worried. You know what? Forget what I said earlier. I just need to know you're all right. Can you call me at least?"

Janet sat at the desk and listened. This voice, pleading and sincere, was much harder to ignore than the voice of anger. She squeezed her eyes shut the way she wanted to squeeze the love for this man out of her heart. But each new message lessened her resolve.

"It's been three hours, Janet. Call me."

"You know I can't sleep with you gone, with no idea if you're at somebody's house or in a car wrapped around a tree somewhere. At least call so I'll know you're alive."

"Is this how the bible teaches you to treat your husband? You're not only going against me, you're going against the word of God."

"Janet, I'm sorry okay? I shouldn't have come home

and taken my anger out on you. It was the alcohol, baby. You know I never beat you when I'm in my right mind. I forgive you for leaving. Will you forgive me?"

The last two messages were breathing and dead air.

You have no more new messages. Saved message.

Janet disconnected the call, and heaved a sigh of relief. All the while she'd listened to messages, Ronald hadn't called. *Maybe since I'm not answering, he'll finally leave me alone.*

Her stomach growled, reminding Janet that she hadn't eaten since dinner the night before. She reached for the room service menu, but jerked her hand back when she heard knocking.

Her heart jumped into her throat as she stared at the door, disbelieving.

No.

"Janet, open the door." Her petrified body refused to move. "Look, I tracked your phone and know you're in here. I'm not leaving and you'd better not call the police. Open this door!"

She briefly considered defying him and calling the police. But even with all he'd done to her the thought of Ronald behind bars was too much to bear. She scanned the room around her. No where to hide. The only escape route was through the front door, the one with an angry, threatening husband on the other side. Prolonging the inevitable would only make him angrier. With shoulders slumped in defeat she crossed the room, removed the security bar and opened the door.

He barged past her. Scanned the room quickly, checked the bathroom. It was on the far side of the room. There was a clear path to the door. Still, Janet didn't think of trying to escape. What was the use? Over and again he'd warned her that there was nowhere she could go where he wouln't find her. No place she could hide that he wouldn't uncover. She'd gathered the courage to leave and his words had proved true. A tracking device on her cell phone? The thought of him resorting to that type of control never crossed her mind. Clearly, it should have.

She watched him, contemplating what measure of punishment he'd use this time.

"Whose room is this? Huh?"

"I-I-It's…it's my room, Ron. I'm the only one here."

"Who got it for you, or gave you the money?" In the time it took for her shoulders to rise and fall, creating a shrug, Ron was in her face with a hand around her throat. "I'm going to ask you one last time. Who helped you get this room? Got dammit you'd better tell me or I'll break your got damn neck."

20

Sunday morning, after Destiny had dressed for service, she called Janet. The call went to voicemail.

"Good morning, Janet. It's Destiny. I'm calling to check up on you and find out if you'd like to be picked up for church. If so, give me a call and we'll have someone come get you. If you'd rather stay there and relax, that's fine, too. Either way, please give me a call. My phone will be off during service, but I'll check messages later. Take care."

Nate joined her in the room next to the garage. "You ready?"

"Yes."

"Where are the kids?"

"Daniel has a slight fever so I'm keeping him home. Sade wanted to stay with her big brother."

"That's a good girl." He opened the door for them to exit. Within moments, they were on the highway, headed for church.

Destiny looked out the window, studying the rocky terrain of the Mojave dessert. The mountain range boasted hues of red, beige, maroon and brown, starkly contrasting against the endless expanse of blue sky dotted with large, fluffy-looking cumulous clouds.

Coming from the lush greenery of the tropics, the land had looked drab and desolate when she first arrived. But travel throughout the city and day trips to places like Red Rock and Lake Mead had helped her realize the beauty of the desert, and appreciate the flowers of life that could bloom there. Of course with some, like roses, there were always thorns.

"Church should be interesting," she said.

"I was just thinking that," Nate replied, turning the stereo volume down.

"You think everyone knows about Ron?"

"Probably. You know the fastest way to spread information is through telephone, telegraph or tell-a-church-member."

Destiny smiled. "Right." She pulled down the visor and checked her makeup. "Are you going to say anything about it?"

Nate shook his head. "With the investigation under way, I think the less said the better."

"I called Janet. Left a message inviting her to church."

Nate glanced over. "You think she'll come?"

"I don't know, but I hope so. Without Ron there judging her every move, she might actually enjoy it."

"Ben made sure all the locks and access codes were changed. Ron turned in his keys, but this was added precaution."

"Do you expect trouble?"

"No. Men like Ron are cowards. All talk. Very little action."

Destiny nodded, remembering the meeting last week with Janet, and the marks Ron's action had left on her face.

They arrived at the church to a palpable tension in

the executive area. Eyes being averted. Whispers behind hands. Fake smiles with their good mornings. Usually here, in the executive office foyer, Nate and Destiny would go their separate ways. She to her office, accompanied by assistants sometimes referred to as ladies-in-waiting, and Nate with his associate ministers for last minute instructions and prayer. But today, Nate firmly held on to her hand.

"I want you with me today, baby."

Her eyes questioned, but she simply said, "Okay."

Some of the frost in the room was melted by Ben and Savannah's warm greeting, the four sharing small talk as they walked down the hall. Reverend Miller and the other ministers stood by Nate's office.

Various greetings were exchanged, with equally diverse attitudes. "A moment before we pray, gentlemen," Nate said, as they prepared to follow him into his office. "Ben. Savannah, come with us."

Nate closed the door. Ben's mouth opened. "I tried to call you, Nate."

"What's going on?"

"The story circulating is that you fired Ron because he caught you stealing money from the church. You knew he was going to the board with the information, so you turned the tables and fired him first to try and make him look bad."

The tactic was so crazy Nate could do nothing but laugh. He walked over to a chair and sat. The others did, too. "So that's the cool breeze we met coming in. The folks out there think I'm the thief. Wow. I guess we know who started that lie."

"Reverend Miller swears up and down that it wasn't him."

"Yeah, the same man who just looked at me like

dammit-I'll-bite-you."

"Like what?" Savannah asked.

"Southern talk," Nate answered with a wave of his hand trying for levity. "That's a little of my mama coming out."

Ben continued to frown. "I bet both of the brothers have been burning up the phone lines, telling these lies to whoever will listen."

"And on you, too, First Lady," Savannah said. She turned compassionate eyes to Destiny. "The other rumor is that you're trying to break up the Miller's marriage; that you talked Janet into leaving her house and going to a hotel."

"So she wouldn't get beaten!" Destiny was exasperated. "I try to save a woman from domestic violence and I'm a homewrecker? Are you kidding me?"

Nate touched Destiny's arm. "Baby, calm down."

"They're lying on us, Nate. And there are people in this church and around the country who'll believe them. How are we going to handle this?"

Nate stood. "You know me. I don't run from fights. I run to them. Let's pray and head inside the sanctuary."

The Thickes and their ministerial entourage entered to a packed house and the sounds of Divine Grace's Mass Choir putting a new twist on a Baptist hymn classic.

Lord, lift me up and let me stand,
By faith, on Heaven's tableland,
A higher plane than I have found,
Lord, plant my feet on higher ground.

As the choir repeated the up-tempo contemporary-sounding refrain, Nate reached for his cordless microphone, stood and encouraged the crowd.

"Does anyone in here want to be lifted? Ask God and I'm a witness that he'll lift you out of the muck and mire, and plant your feet on higher ground. I dare you to stand up, open up your mouth and let your petition be known to God."

The sanctuary responded. Hands were raised across the room. Destiny stood as well, praising and appraising. She saw the faithful and the curious. The skeptical and the sanctified. Most had come to hear the gospel, but those who'd heard Ronald's malicious lies were there to witness what had been gossiped firsthand.

The song ended. Nate stood at the podium. "Somebody give the Lord a hand of praise."

The applause died down. Nate scanned the room feeling an energy of anticipation, people waiting for something to happen, or for what he'd say.

"How many of you believe there are no accidents?" Various members responded. "I believe that, too. I prayed before coming before you, as I do before entering any pulpit anywhere. Last week was a difficult one for both me and the ministry and just now I learned of yet another twist to the plot. I prayed, asking what I should say. Or if I should say anything at all. And if I was to speak, what words should I use? Should I defend? Deny? Explain? What? I didn't get an answer. And then I entered the sanctuary and..."

The double doors at the back of the church flew open. A couple entered the church's main edifice and made their way down the center aisle. An usher hurried to escort them to open seats. Murmurs preceded Ronald and Janet Miller like rose petals dropped down the aisle of a bride.

"I entered the sanctuary and heard the choir," Nate

continued, regaining his composure before the latecomers reached the third row and sat. "When I heard the words of the song being sung, I knew that God was answering me at that very moment. Because the words of that old Baptist hymn, particularly the third verse, are both my prayer and today's message."

He looked directly at a defiant Ronald, his gaze unflinching, then at Janet, sitting meekly beside him, with softer eyes. His voice was strong as he moved across the pulpit. Those listening hung on to every word penned as the third verse of the age-old hymnal. "I want to live above the world, though Satan's darts at me are hurled. For faith has caught the joyful sound. The song of saints on higher ground."

*

Destiny had watched the Miller's grand entrance in shock—Ronald cutting an impressive figure in a tailored black suit. Janet walking beside him in pale pink and pumps. The same woman who two nights ago had called Destiny a blessing, who'd promised not to take Ronald's calls. And now rumor had it that she was at fault? Ruining their marriage? Destiny had never been so angry.

It took great effort, but she made it through the service with poise and grace. Though if asked, she couldn't have repeated a word of her husband's sermon. The benediction barely over, Ben was at Nate's side.

"Boss, considering the, um, circumstances, perhaps we should skip you and Destiny staying to greet the guests and head back to the office."

"Absolutely not." Nate smiled and waved as if nothing was amiss. "We're going to greet people like we do every Sunday."

That's exactly what happened. The pastor and first lady stepped down and to the right of the raised platform. A line of visitors and well-wishers had already begun to form. Ben texted on his phone while flanking the pastor. Savannah stood next to Destiny. Nate greeted each guest warmly. He shook hands and pinched a few baby cheeks. Destiny smiled and gave hugs. The line continued to grow. When Destiny looked up several minutes later, she met the eyes of Ronald Miller, now in line. Janet was beside him. When they were three couples back, two church security guards appeared in Destiny's peripheral vision. Her smile slipped, then faded altogether. Knots formed in her gut. She felt a subtle touch, Nate's hand on the small of her back. A reassuring pat, but she felt the message. *I'm here. I've got you. Stay strong.*

She hugged the woman in front of her and thanked her for coming, heard Nate laugh at something the husband said.

Two couples between the Millers and Thickes.

"Rev. Thicke!" said a woman carrying a book and a bible. "It's such a pleasure to meet you!" The excitement in the woman's voice brought back Destiny's smile. "I saw you on TV and bought your book. It is really inspiring. Can you sign it for me?"

"Absolutely," Nate said. He agreed to her request for a picture, too.

One couple. Members. Older. Well-dressed.

"Pastor, my mother-in-law, his mother, is having surgery tomorrow. Her name is Betty Clarksdale. She's eighty-seven pastor, and we're worried sick. Can you please say a prayer for her?"

Nate took the woman's hand, his expression sincere. "Jesus is a healer, beloved. I entrust Sister Betty

Clarksdale to His care, believing that He is well able to guide the surgeons, bind the sickness, and bring total healing. In Jesus's name."

"Thank you, pastor! God bless you!"

The Millers stepped forward.

To some people watching, this was just another couple greeting the man of God and his lovely wife. They wouldn't know that two men in blue suits a few feet away were armed church security. Or that five more watched closely, and three guarded doors. Most would not assume that mild-mannered Ben Harvey, a slight five-nine and one sixty soaking wet held a black belt in karate and could drop a man twice his size. They wouldn't. But Ronald would, and did. As he glanced around, Destiny saw the realization dawn in his eyes. He also noticed how many people were watching. Destiny shifted her focus to Janet, who had not looked her way.

"Rev. Thicke!" Ronald's greeting was forced and said too loudly. He made a show of holding out his hand. Nate met the false welcome with an act of his own.

"Praise the Lord, Deacon Miller! It's a good day to be in God's house."

"There's no other place I'd be on a Sunday than in my church. Me and my wife." Ronald leaned closer and lowered his voice. "Yours butted in where she doesn't belong. Big mistake."

Nate dropped his voice to a whisper, pushed harsh words between a bright smile. "Not as big as the lies you've told."

Ron glowered at Nate, eyes blazing. A security guard took a step forward. Nate's subtle headshake stopped the advance.

Destiny missed this exchange because of the one she had with Janet. After continuing to be ignored, Destiny stepped over and hugged her.

"Whatever he said or did to make you come back," she hastily whispered. "I'm still praying for you."

Just as Janet opened her mouth to speak, Ronald interrupted. "Lady Destiny, ravishing as always." He subtly moved Janet out of the way and held out his hand. Destiny pointedly ignored it, and him. The message was clear. He'd been dismissed. Instead she looked again at Janet and was met with sorrow-filled eyes. In that moment she knew that anything negative said about her had been at Ron's direction and that Janet standing beside him was not by choice.

One minute, two tops, and the exchange ended. The Millers walked down a side aisle and out of the building. Destiny felt Nate relax but knew he wasn't fooled. She wasn't either. Whatever plan Ronald had for coming to church had failed. But his pride had been wounded. He would seek revenge.

21

It had been three days since the blow-up. Seventy-two hours since Princess had argued against Kelvin going to LA and, when he insisted, refused to go along. She hadn't heard from him and had refused to call. If he wanted to dance to Fawn's melodramatic tune, fine. But he would dance alone.

Princess jumped off the couch, tired of thinking. Exhausted from being angry. Even Tai had taken Kelvin's side. "That child is innocent in this," she'd reasoned. Yes, but so was her husband. And so was she! Tai had gone back to San Diego and taken Kiara, suggesting her daughter pray and do some soul searching. Being by herself sounded good at the time. But it left the house too quiet and empty, and left her with little to do. Yesterday, she'd tried shopping, but her girlfriends were busy and it was no fun alone. This morning she'd tried to focus on work, shows being taped in the next few weeks. Every topic somehow tied into home, marriage, relationships or kids. The very things she didn't want to think about.

"I've got to get out this house. It's driving me crazy." She ran upstairs, changed into jeans and a tee, grabbed her purse and was out the door. With no destination in mind, she got into her car and headed out the driveway. Ten minutes later she was on I-17, trying without success to run away from herself.

The phone rang. Destiny. *Yay...a distraction!* "Hey, girl."

"Hey, Princess. You busy?"

"Nope, on the highway."

"Oh, where are you headed?"

"I have no idea."

"Okay." Said in a way to suggest it wasn't okay at all.

"Kelvin and I got into it over the weekend."

"I'm sorry, Princess. Did he take losing the game out on you?"

"I wish that was the reason. That, I would have understood."

"So what was the problem, or should I not ask?"

"He went to LA to check on his son."

Silence, and then, "And you're upset about it?"

"Yes, because I didn't want him to go. I told him that Fawn was playing games, Kelly was adjusting to a new temp daddy, and I didn't think there was anything seriously wrong. But did he listen to me? No. He fired up the private jet, as if he couldn't wait for the next commercial flight out, and was off to LA on a rescue mission."

"He didn't want you to go along?"

"Sure, he asked me. I wasn't going to be a part of that madness. Ever since she's had that child, Fawn has made Kelvin jump through hoops. Even when he found out the whole truth about Kelly, he still manned up and has taken care of that child from the day he was born. He has another child now, one he saw come into the world and knows for sure is his. Kiara should be his focus. Let

Fawn and his money take care of that boy."

"You don't mean that. You're just mad."

"Yes, I'm angry. Because I know what he's thinking. Kelvin wants Kelly to live here, with us."

"Why, because of Fawn's new boyfriend?"

"That's the excuse he'll use. But he's mentioned it before. He found out the guy's name and looked him up online. He probably has some type of record, like every other Black man in America. One that probably includes violence. That's the only possible rationale for Kelvin's uncharacteristic behavior. That and a feeling he had," she said, her voice filled with disdain.

"That must have been some kind of feeling, for him to fly to LA."

"The only thing I've felt is Fawn and her bullshit. She's probably been planning this all along, getting Kelvin to raise that boy. Since the pregnancy didn't result in her getting the man, she wants to get rid of the child."

"Then Kiara and her brother could grow up together. Would that be so bad?"

"Seriously, Destiny? You're asking me if I'd be fine raising Fawn's child? The woman who's caused me nothing but grief from the time I laid eyes on her?"

"Not just Fawn's child, but Kelvin's, too." Princess remained silent. "I've heard you talk about Kelly and know how much you love him. And you've told me yourself that Fawn wasn't maternal. Maybe this is God's way of working everything out."

"Easy for you to say."

"Because I'm thinking of the child, of Kelly."

"Answer me this. Would you feel the same way if we were talking about a child Melody had with Nate? If during one of their sexual romps they made a little Nate?

Maybe the one that was caught on tape? Would you still be this loving, compassionate woman thinking only of the child? Having to spend the next ten or so years looking at Melody's face at the dinner table? No, you wouldn't. You'd be pissed and trying to think of an alternate solution. Just like me."

"You know what, Princess. You're right. Not that I'd automatically feel the same way as you do, but I've never been in your position and don't know how I'd feel. Or what I'd do. I probably feel the same about Melody as you do about Fawn. So having to deal with her on a regular basis would no doubt be difficult. Adding a child to the mix would make it harder still. I apologize for sounding judgmental, and will support you no matter what happens or what you guys decide to do."

"Thanks, Destiny. I didn't mean to blow up on you. This whole situation has me stressed out."

"You should go to a spa, get a massage. A mud bath. Do some aromatherapy and get taken away on a jasmine cloud."

Princess smiled for the first time all day. "That's something Mom would say, but you know what? I'm headed toward Sedona. One of Mom's favorite spas is there. So I might do just that. Enough about me, though. How's life in Sin City?"

"Challenging."

"Still dealing with that guy, the wife beater?"

"Yes, and what began as my effort to stop domestic violence has turned into him labeling me a homewrecker."

"Stop!"

Destiny filled her in on Sunday's events. "For all of my sister to sister intentions, his wife is still a captive."

"Sister to sister?"

"That's the working title of the speech I'm giving at the conference. You know, the whole sisterhood theme and how we are our sister's keeper."

"Yes but we can only help so much. At some point, she's going to have to help herself."

"I think the lies came from her husband. But you're right. She'd left their house and was at a hotel. No matter what he said to her, she didn't have to go back. She made a choice. So I'm done with it."

"Not if they stay at that church, you're not. There's no way you'll be able to ignore that situation, and the members will definitely be paying attention. You'd think a man like that would want to find somewhere else to worship, a place where he could feel important again."

"Nate says to give it time and no energy, that Ron will stop huffing and puffing when he's being ignored."

"Lack of attention didn't work with Fawn so good luck with that."

"Why do we attract the crazies? Either us or our men?"

"I don't know, but it's time for a change."

The women didn't know it yet, but a change was coming.

22

On a Friday afternoon two weeks later Nate strolled into the house, whistling. He walked into the room that had been converted into Destiny's closet and found her standing over a pile of clothes.

"Pack your bags, my lady," he said after a hug and a kiss. "I'm taking you away."

"You're home early. It's not even three o'clock."

"I know. I want to get ahead of the rush hour traffic."

She pulled back from his embrace to look at him. "And sounding so sound happy, too. What's going on?"

"It's Friday, my date with destiny night, that's what."

"All of this good mood over a date with me?"

"Absolutely. Two weeks ago we were in Phoenix. Followed by a week of Miller madness and the restraining order we filed."

"I still don't know if that was necessary."

"We don't know that it wasn't, either."

Following Ronald's whispered veiled threat that Sunday, Nate had insisted they go to the police station and put the incident on record. Nate assumed the order had been served on him. Neither Ron, his brother Roy nor either wife had been seen at Divine Grace since.

"Last Friday was the board meeting at church that ran until midnight. I've been late coming home every night this week and you have not complained. Dealing with all the ministry madness has made me remiss in my husbandly duties. That's a situation I plan to rectify. Tonight." He noticed the pile of clothes. "What are you doing?"

"Going through my closet for items I no longer wear. SOS is doing a clothing drive for several women's shelters that the organization supports. An email went out reminding everyone attending the conference to either bring clothing with them or ship it to a central address."

"That's good, baby. You can finish tomorrow. For now, you need to go throw some toiletries into a bag along with a nice dress for dinner. Other than that you'll be naked so one dress is all you'll need."

"Oh, it's like that, huh?" She wrapped her arms around his neck.

His arm slid around her waist. "It's exactly like that."

Less than an hour later, Destiny was on her way to an unknown destination. When she asked, Nate's answer was simple. "You'll know when you get there."

As he reached the I-515 onramp, she decided to relax and enjoy the ride.

For the first fifteen or so minutes, the conversation was sparse. Nate had set the stereo to a customized smooth jazz station. Destiny listened and tried not to think at all. Once they were outside of the metro area, she took off her shoes, reclined her seat and exhaled.

"Thanks, babe." She reached over and placed her hand atop his. "I didn't even know I needed a getaway but now that we're on it…thanks."

"You're welcome. It's something we both needed. And," he turned down the volume on the stereo, "there are several reasons for my good mood."

"I knew it was something. Tell me!"

"Sometime this afternoon Ronald Miller will be arrested."

This news was a jaw dropper. The Millers weren't at church the previous Sunday. For a solid week, their names had not come up at all.

"Janet pressed charges?"

"Hardly," Nate said, giving her a look. "The bank contacted Mrs. Strong's nephew, who was so upset about what happened that he immediately called for an investigation. The examiner confirmed that Ronald withdrew the money, almost seventy-five grand in the past three years. His name was on the account but Charles, the nephew, believes his aunt was either coerced or duped into adding it."

"Can they prove it? And unless or until they do, how can he be arrested for taking money from an account with his name on it?"

"There is no record of this account anywhere in the paperwork obtained by Mrs. Strong's estate, even though she allegedly opened the account. As a signee, Ron should have disclosed this information or made Charles aware of the account, at the very least. Because he not only kept the account hidden but continued to draw funds from it after her death the authorities had reasonable cause to place him under arrest. He'll post bond and get out, but the arrest gives prosecutors access to all of his bank statements, tax returns, business transactions, everything. Before it's all over, Janet may go down as well."

"She knew about it?"

Nate shrugged. "That remains to be seen. But a dummy organization was created to stash the siphoned funds. It's called The Rutherford House. Incorporation papers list Janet as one of the officers. Rutherford is her maiden name."

"Oh. My. God. That's crazy!" Destiny gazed out of the window, absorbing Nate's update. "I doubt she had anything to do with it," she said at last. "Even though she went back to her husband I think I got to see the real Janet, the woman she'd be if not with Ron. Not often, and not for long, but a couple times I caught a glimpse of her. And I liked her."

"Baby, you did what you could."

"I know."

"Okay, now that I've shared that bit of news, I'm going to exchange my preacher hat for my pimp suit."

"Ha! Is that right?"

"Yes. And you're going to lose that first lady armor and become my lady of the night."

Destiny ran a hand up his thigh, rested it on his healthy package and gave a little squeeze. "All right then, Mister Big. I'm ready to work for you all night long."

The couple's sole intention was to enjoy each other. And they did. Dinner was great. Dessert was better and involved more than food. The hotel ambiance was posh, the surrounding scenery, stunning. The next evening as they headed home it was a smooth groove for Destiny and Nate all the way down the Nevada highway. A good thing, because just up ahead they would find themselves smack dab in the intersection of crazy, confusion, drama and mess.

23

The following Tuesday Destiny had breakfast with the kids before heading to Divine Grace for a meeting with Savannah, who'd just returned from two weeks in Turks and Caicos. Destiny couldn't wait to catch up. The two women hadn't had a chance to talk in depth since the restraining order incident. She was sure Savannah had island news, probably just enough to make Destiny homesick and ready for the Thicke's planned vacation after the holidays.

Halfway there, her phone rang. "Good morning, Mom!"

"Sounds like a very good morning for somebody."

"Yes it is. On Friday, Nate and I got away for some much-needed couple time. We came back late Saturday night. And then yesterday we had a guest preacher. He's one of several Nate is looking at to replace the one who left. He's in the process of reorganizing his entire staff. After what happened with the Millers he wants to make certain that everyone around him is in line with his plans for this ministry. If not, they have to go. Period. He has put his foot down and made it very clear. Finally, he feels he has a board that is fully committed to what we feel God has called us to do. Even though we've been here for a year, it's like now we can begin to really move forward and build the ministry we had in mind when we arrived. The dead weight, and the naysayers and the stubborn ones in the old guard are either already gone or planning to leave. So we're excited."

"I am too, Destiny. I tried to hide it but Mark and I have been so worried about you guys, especially when you told me the couple showed up at church. I thought, oh no, that's not good. Mark and I prayed, literally got on our knees and asked God to protect you. Because men like that...you just never know about them. And even though his wife asked you to intervene, well, I'm just glad that's over and they're gone."

"That makes two of us. So anyway, I'm headed to the church to meet with Savannah. Can't wait to hear all about their vacation and then she and I are going to outline plans to start an SOS chapter in Las Vegas."

"Very nice."

"Lady Viv is hyped as well and has promised to come down as often as needed to help us make it a successful, productive branch. I'm sure there are lots of women in and around the metropolitan area who can benefit from the types of programs Sanctity of Sisterhood provides."

"Destiny, it sounds like you're going to be very busy. And I know you love working with your husband. But be sure and carve out some Destiny time. Not church-related or mommy-related but activities that nourish your own soul."

"That's good advice, Mom. Thanks. What about you? What's going on in the Big Easy?" They talked until Destiny reached Divine Grace. Savannah had also just arrived. She waved as Destiny pulled in beside her. "No, you didn't tell me that Kat met someone! Oh my goodness. I'll call you tonight. Oh, and glad you're still working on my song!"

Destiny got out of her car and gave Savannah a big hug. "Look at you with that island glow! I'm so jealous!"

"Hello, Lady!"

"Come in and tell me everything. I've got stuff to share too. All good."

*

While life was all good for Destiny, Ronald's situation had gone from bad to increasingly worse. Accused of stealing. Kicked out of church. Served a restraining order. Charged with grand theft. This Class B felony was punishable by fines, restitution and up to ten years in jail. His life ruined, and who was to blame? Nate and Destiny Thicke.

Ronald sat at a corner booth in Prestige, a daily event for the past few weeks, sipping a Remy Martin Louis XIII cognac, neat. Access to the two-thousand dollar bottle of France's finest came courtesy of the woman who had done more than pique his interest and stiffen his soldier. The woman who not only might have the means to get him out of this situation, but may become the partner he needed in a scheme he was close to implementing before getting busted. Melody Anderson might be young, but she was not innocent or naïve. He'd have to tread with caution but not moving forward with some type of money-making plan was not an option.

He sat back and casually observed the specialists. Their actions were classy and understated, as if holding a mid-day conversation with butt-cheeks out and breasts barely covered was the most normal thing to do in the world. The strategic placement of tables, plants and figurines combined with dim lighting, made lap dances performed in the main room semi-private affairs. Many had offered, but Ron had declined all lap dance routines. He preferred a more intimate type of tango, one with no clothes, no audience and a device to cause pain.

Melody emerged from the back office area. He watched her saunter through the club's main floor, striking and confident. The conservative tan pantsuit she wore masked a fire he knew she possessed deep within her. A fire for money, power, sex. It's not something she'd told him. He recognized it because he saw it in himself.

"Good afternoon, Mr. Miller."

"Hello, Melody. You're looking super sexy today, as always."

"And you are brooding, as always," she said with a smile as she slid into the booth. "You must have a lot of serious stuff on your mind."

"I'm a Black man in America. That's serious business."

"The man trying to bring you down?" A message came through on Melody's cell phone. She picked it up, returned the text and continued to browse.

"Actually the man is treating me just fine. It's my own trying to bring me down."

Melody shook her head. "That's too bad."

Ron took a sip of his cognac, studying Melody and wondering how to broach the subject of her becoming an "investor." He was just about to come from a business expansion angle when she suddenly stopped scrolling and used her fingers to widen the screen.

"I don't believe it."

"I imagined a worldly woman like you would believe

just about anything."

"Pretty much," she said with a chuckle. "But coincidences are always surprising. A friend just sent me an email about an old pastor friend I used to, let's say consult, who has a church here now."

The tumbler near Ron's lips was slowly lowered to the table. *Was there a chance that…no…I'm sure there's no chance at all.*

There was only one way to find out for sure. He adopted a light tone. "Please don't take this the wrong way, but you don't strike me as a church girl."

"No offense taken. The business that Nate and I handled was in the bedroom not the sanctuary. But that's before he pissed me off and I send his arrogant ass running to an island to hide from my rage."

Ronald maintained a cool façade but his mind whirled. It was almost inconceivable that she was talking about Nate Thicke. But his ex-pastor was indeed arrogant and had come here from an island, two qualities that didn't fit most people. But that she knew Nate and disliked him? Impossible. But he pressed on anyway.

"Out of the country?" Melody nodded. "Wow, baby girl. You've got some kind of clout to be able to chase away a man of God."

"It doesn't take much. A man of God is still a man made of flesh. His flesh is very weak."

Seeing no way to handle this subtly, he decided to come clean. "You wouldn't happen to be talking about Nate Thicke would you?"

Melody's eyes widened. "You know him?"

Ronald nodded. "Sadly, yes."

"Why, sadly? He try to hit on you, too?"

"Hell, no!"

"Calm down, Mr. Miller. That was a joke. But you

said that as if there is no love lost between the two of you."

"I trusted him in business. He's a thief. And his wife has a thing for me, and tried to break up my marriage."

"Destiny?"

"You know her, too?"

"I've known her for years. We attended the same high school."

"In Texas?"

"Louisiana."

"Is that where she's from?"

Melody shrugged. "So she finally got tired of being a one-man woman, huh? She used to brag about Nate being her one and only when there's probably been a whole basketball team inside that snatch."

"Damn, Melody." He said this as if to admonish her, but his eyes twinkled.

"Just calling it like I see it, especially with her always trying to act better than me. I'd love to see her pulled off of that high horse she rides."

"Nate is the one I'd like to take down."

"If you want to wreck Nate, hurt Destiny."

Ronald sat back, and let that thought sink in. "How would you do that, you know, hypothetically speaking?"

Based on her own experience, Melody's answer was quick. "I'd make a little video and have it accidentally go viral." She laughed heartily.

Ronald got hard.

"Miss Poised and Perfect Destiny would drop dead in disgrace," Melody continued, still laughing. "But that could never happen so I guess she's safe."

"Nothing's impossible."

"Taping Destiny is. I'm sure Nate has her on lockdown, with church security watching like a hawk.

They've already had one scandal with cameras and have probably taken every precaution that there won't be anymore."

"I could make that happen," Ronald stated confidently.

"How? Sneak into her home and install a camera?"

"No need to share the details. But I guarantee I could make your wish come true."

"Quit bullshitting me," Melody teased. "You're a businessman, not a criminal."

"How much is it worth to you?"

"Worth? As in money?" He nodded. "Okay, I see you're enjoying this fantasy. I'll play along. Let's say…a thousand."

"Ha! Okay, now you're the one bullshitting. That's okay, though. You're playing and I'm serious." Ron eyed her over his tumbler as he took a swig.

"What did Nate do to you for you to hate him so much?"

"I told you, already. He messed with my money, cost me a lucrative church contract. I hate that motherfucker. But that's all right. I know you're taken care of, don't have your own money to do as you please."

"Mr. Miller, I have plenty of money."

"Really? Then how much would you pay me to show Destiny that she's no better than you?"

Not that Ronald cared, but he was desperate. If this was the fastest way for him to get his hands on some real money, then this is the road he'd go down.

"How much would it take?"

"Probably more than you can handle, baby girl."

"Let me be the judge of that. How much?"

Numbers pinged all around Ronald's head. Too and she'd walk away. Too little and he'd leave money on the table.

"There's a couple ways this could happen. You could pay me ten thousand outright, or say…a couple thousand now and a percentage of whatever that tape will prove to be worth."

"Oh. So, you'd sell the tape instead of putting it out for free?"

"Why not? Nate Thicke is a national bestseller, a multimillionaire from what I hear. He would probably pay almost anything to prevent a video like that from ending up on the internet."

Melody's eyes shined with excitement. "Spoken like a true businessman. I didn't even think of that. But, wait. Why do you need my money? Why would you want it? Just make the tape and take the haul."

"That's true."

"I don't believe you, anyway. You're all man, Mr. Miller, there's no mistaking that. But to cross Nate Thicke?" Melody shook her head. "I don't think so."

"Then you're not as good a judge of character as I thought."

"Tell you what. If you're as badass as you say and can get Destiny on tape, I'll pay you ten thousand dollars and you can keep all the earnings from the tape. How's that?"

"Are you serious?"

Melody laughed again, and then shrugged. "Sure, but to get the money I have to have proof."

much

"I'll get your proof, no problem. You just have my money ready because when it comes to business, I don't fuck around." Ronald held out his hand, his eyes narrow and black. "Do we have a deal for real?"

Melody hesitated, and shrugged again. "Deal."

Ronald watched her walk away, a plot already forming. He wasn't worried about whether or not Melody was serious. They'd made a deal so he'd get his money out of her. One way or another, payment would be made.

24

"Are the two of you still fighting?" Tai asked her daughter, just seconds after answering the phone.

"No."

"Good."

"We're just not talking."

"Princess! That's not good either."

Princess knew her mother was right. Marriages with partners who didn't communicate rarely worked well. Or lasted long. Staying together was hard enough even when conversation flowed. Still, mutual silence had basically been the situation between her and Kelvin for the past few weeks, ever since he'd come back home and spoken the six words she'd most dreaded.

I want to raise my son.

"I can't believe you've let it go on this long!"

Princess turned off the TV she wasn't even watching and marched out of the room. "Me? What about him?" she asked, stomping up the stairs. "He hasn't tried talking either, still staying in one of the guest rooms. And that's when he decides to finally come home from wherever he is at one or two in the morning. I don't think I should be made to feel like a bad person because I told my truth. I don't want to raise another woman's child."

"Another woman's child or specifically Fawn's child?"

"Can't say I'm proud of it but my disdain for Fawn plays a huge role. If forced to raise Kelly, have the reminder of her under my roof twenty-four/seven, there would be resentment and anger. Frustration and feelings that would undoubtedly bleed into how I treated him. So, is it better to say how I really feel up front or act like everything is hunky dory and bring a child into a toxic environment?"

"It's better for you to act like the daughter your mother raised and start thinking about someone besides yourself."

"I am thinking about someone else. I'm thinking about Kelly."

"After what Kelvin shared with you, if you were thinking about Kelly you and Kelvin would be in an attorney's office right now working out a way to bring Kelly into your home. If you were thinking about Kelly you'd be working on forgiveness and compassion, two acts that would help change your attitude. Now, I know you probably don't like or agree with what I'm saying. But you asked."

"You're right, Mom. I don't agree with what you're saying. I'm getting off the phone."

"I still love you, Princess. But I can't support you when you're wrong."

Princess disconnected the call, went to the master suite and tossed the phone on to the king-sized bed. Why was it that everyone could see Kelvin's point and no one could see hers? She'd talked to her mom, Aunt Viv and Destiny. All of them felt she should do the right thing, and the right thing was to take the boy. The only one who even admitted they'd hesitate was her college bestie Joanie, who said she didn't know if she'd be able to love the son of a woman she hated.

Opening the French doors that led to a balcony overlooking Paradise Valley and beyond it to Piestewa Peak, it was hot, close to a hundred degrees. Princess barely noticed. Her anger was even hotter. She walked over to a shaded, air-conditioned alcove, sat on a chaise, and thought back to the phone call between her and Kelvin that set off the standoff.

*

It was around two in the afternoon, four days after Kelvin had acted on impulse and flew to LA.

"About time you called."

"Hey, Princess." Silence. "I apologize for not calling. I was angry that you didn't come with me. It felt like you didn't care."

"We have another child that needs to be taken care of, or did you forget that?"

"Your mom was there, Princess. She would have watched Kiara, in fact, Kiara is with her now."

"How do you know?"

"Does it matter? I know."

"Did my mom call you?"

"I called Bella so I could speak with my daughter and she told me, all right? And you'd better not say anything to her about it. I don't want her in the middle of a mess you caused."

"I'm not the one who hopped on a plane to check on an ex-girlfriend's son."

"When you look at Kelly is Fawn all you see?" Princess didn't answer. "It's a good thing I came here. My gut was right, Princess. Kelly's behavior changed for a reason. He was being traumatized, Princess. Gerald's got two sons, both older than him. They moved in when he did and were acting like bullies. Like it was their house. They've taken Kelly's stuff, beaten him up, and threatened him with worse. Fawn allowed this man and his kids to move in and take over a condo I purchased."

"Who told you this? I can't imagine Fawn did."

"No, she didn't. I hired a private investigator, a woman who specializes in handling child cases. Her name is Julie. She snooped around their complex and found a next-door neighbor more than ready to talk, a woman who more than once had almost called the police over loud music and noise. She complained to Julie about arguments, fighting, all kind of stuff happening over there. When Julie tried to talk to Fawn and see Kelly, no one answered the door. So last night I called Fawn, told her I was in town and that if she'd bring my son to the hotel, I'd give her the money."

"You and Fawn in a hotel room? Just what I need to hear."

"We met in the lobby. Kelly spent the night. It took a while, but he finally opened up and told me what else was going on."

"So being in a hotel room did it? That was the magic that made him talk after all this time? After we questioned him here repeatedly and he denied anything was wrong?"

"Have you heard anything I've said? My son was traumatized. This shit is serious. And it's real. It took a long time and a lot of reassurance that nothing would happen if he told me the whole truth. I shared what the detective told me and convinced him that as his father, I would love him no matter what. He finally told me everything, even though the twelve-year-old had threatened to kill him if that ever happened.

"He had them doing things, Princess. The twelve-year-old had his eight-year-old brother and Kelly doing stuff that shouldn't happen with kids. You feel me?"

"Are you saying he was sexually molested?"

"He made the two younger boys play with each other, and not on the playground. What would you call it?"

"If by play you mean touching, it may not have been sexual. Kids are curious like that."

"Think what you want but Kelly is not going back there. I've made up my mind."

"Kelvin, if what you believe is true then I agree that something definitely needs to be done. I'd start with giving Fawn an ultimatum that it's either her man leaves and takes his kids or she loses the house."

"The condo is hers, Princess. Paid for in cash with the deed in her name. And as to whether or not this is true, I believe Kelly. If you'd seen him while he was telling the story, you'd believe him, too."

A long pause and then, "I'm sorry, Kelvin. Abuse is horrible, no matter what kind. No child should ever have to deal with that, especially Kelly."

"Thank you. I was beginning to wonder who was this cold, unfeeling woman I was talking to and where was my wife?"

"I don't mean to sound callous and apologize for not being more understanding. It's just that...a challenging situation just became even more difficult, and there are no easy solutions. Dealing with Fawn always brings out the worst in me. You know that. Where is Kelly now?"

"Over to his aunt's house. I told Fawn if he went back to her home I was calling social services immediately. It won't be for long, though. I've been talking to my lawyer nonstop since I found out what happened and I think we may have a plan."

Princess was silent, feeling it was a plan she didn't want to hear. But he told her anyway.

"We're prepared to offer her a seven-figure monetary amount to give up her rights to Kelly."

"Give up her rights? And then what?"

"And then Kelly comes home to Arizona, Princess. I'm raising my son."

*

Recalling that conversation brought back other memories. Another life, another child, and another selfish decision. And then there was the son she lost while pregnant with Kiara, the brother who would have been her twin. Now this situation and a son who needed her. Could she get past the fact of Fawn being Kelly's mother and truly love him as she would her own? And if she couldn't, what then? Would Kelvin leave her? Would he allow Kelly to remain in potential danger? Would he call social services, a move that might place Kelly in foster care? And would her conscious be clear if any of those scenarios occurred? Princess pressed fingers against her temples. She had a headache, brought on by too much thinking and the opinions shared by loved ones that echoed in her head.

Kiara and her brother could grow up together.

I'm raising my son.

I want to raise my son.

If you were thinking about Kelly, you would be working on forgiveness and compassion.

When you look at Kelly is Fawn all you see?

It's better for you to act like the daughter your mother raised and start thinking about someone besides yourself.

I want to raise my son.

I've heard you talk about Kelly. You love that child.

The twelve-year-old had threatened to kill Kelly if he ever told.

I was beginning to wonder who was this cold, unfeeling woman I was talking to and where was my wife?

I still love you, Princess. But I can't support you when you're wrong.

I'm raising my son.

Princess released an exasperated breath as she got up and went back into the house. She slowly walked the hallway leading to the two story-living room. Her hands glided along the framed art on the wall, exquisite works worth millions, bought less for show and more for their investment value. She reached a second story landing that boasted spiral staircases on either side and gazed at the massive room below her—the ten-foot circle top double doors with stainless steel glass, a foyer larger than some people's bedroom and a Mediterranean-inspired living room created by one of America's top interior designers. Floor to ceiling windows offered panoramic views and the fireplace, one of seven, was large enough to roast a whole pig on a spit. All of this grandeur in a space of more than ten-thousand feet.

Yet you have no room for a child?

The thought hit Princess with such conviction that her legs almost gave out. She sat on the floor, her head in her hands as a truthful examination of her heart brought tears. She had allowed past hurt, deep anger, smoldering resentment and a sense of entitlement overshadow the daughter of God she was at her core. That woman would never allow a child to remain in danger, or anyone for that matter, if she could help them be saved. Tai was right, Princess realized, as more tears flowed. And so was Aunt Viv. Destiny, too. She'd grown up hearing about the God of second chances and knew it was true. She'd gotten two or three. So maybe it was time to pay it forward, and help a little boy with his second chance. Maybe it was her chance to love a son on earth, instead of mourning the ones in heaven.

Princess wiped her eyes and slowly rose to her feet. It was time to find her husband, and bring Kelly home.

25

Ronald waited a week to set his plan in motion. There was no room for error and there would be no second takes. Every detail had been thought out and researched with the utmost of care. His was the brain behind most of it and while she acted ambivalently, Melody had proved useful, too. She'd told him about a condo owned by a European businessman, the space where he'd carry out his plan. More importantly, she'd shared where the businessman hid the spare key.

Failure was not an option. The six to seven-figure payoff he believed Nate would pay for the video would change his life. He'd divorce Janet, leave the area, and get a new identity. Divine Grace and the felony charge would all be behind him. Ahead of him would be the rest of a wonderful life. But the money wasn't even the best part. The biggest thrill of what he was about to pull off was finally getting a taste of Destiny Thicke. He planned to sex Nate's whore until he was good and satisfied, and then teach her what happened when a real man got crossed. Nate would know it happened and not be able to do a thing about it. Why? Because if he were ever implicated the video would be released. Sure he could release it whether or not that happened. Nate didn't need to know that, though. For the first time since moving to Nevada, Nate would just have to trust him. Ronald would have all the cards. And the deck was stacked in his favor. There was only one piece of the plan outside of his control. Five minutes, or ten, where it all could go wrong. But it wouldn't. It couldn't. Or there would be hell to pay.

Ronald reached the neighborhood where the condo was located. He circled the block, then drove his rented black Toyota into the alley and pulled into the detached garage. After checking the backyards for signs of life and seeing none, he quickly crossed the mulch and gravel that passed for a lawn and slipped through the patio door he had earlier unlocked.

He walked into the living room with his accomplice.

"It's time to do this. Are you ready?"

"Yes."

"Remember how we practiced. Just relax and be yourself."

"Okay."

"Don't mess up."

"I won't."

"You'd better not. Do you hear me? This is your one and only warning."

*

Destiny sat in her office at Divine Grace, sipping chai tea from her favorite shop. Now that plans were underway for a local SOS chapter she was familiarizing herself with the church's female members. A core group would be selected to learn the organization's tenets and then actively recruit women willing to join. This she worked on while handling her usual appointments with those experiencing challenges or in need of special prayer. It had been a busy and productive day, but she was at the end of it. Her last appointment was in an hour, at four o'clock. Instead of going home afterward she and Savannah were going to discuss the day over dinner, then return in time for mid-week praise and worship and bible study.

A light tap on her office door took her attention away from the list Savannah had compiled.

"Hey, Lady."

"Yes, Savannah?"

"Check out this new restaurant over by the strip. This ad says they serve fresh seafood daily, buffet style, for only $19.95."

"Hungry much?" Destiny asked, laughing.

"You know I'm trying to shed these ten pounds I picked up in the two weeks I spent on the island. I have a special shake for breakfast and lunch. Dinner is my only meal. I'm ready to eat that desk out there."

"Are you sure you can last until after my appointment?"

"I might but if you come out and a corner of my desk is gnawed off, you'll know that drinking tons of water as they suggested wasn't enough." The office phone rang. "Let me get this. Hopefully, it's Margaret canceling so we can leave right now!"

Destiny smiled and shook her head as she went back to the list. A short time later she switched from that to revising her SOS speech. With Nate's help it was definitely better. But it still didn't feel comfortable. To her, it didn't flow.

Savannah entered the office again, her eyes twinkling.

"That was Margaret."

"Yes, honey, and she's way out in Summerlin with

a flat tire."

"Oh, no."

"Oh, yes. She's called road service but there's a thirty- to forty-five-minute wait." Savannah did a little holy dance. "Won't God do it?"

"Girl, you know you're wrong."

"Jesus understands where a sister is coming from. Seafood was his favorite food, too."

"And you know this because?"

"Because he fed fish to the five thousand. If his name had been Jerome instead of Jesus that crowd would have gotten greens, cornbread and some golden fried chicken!"

Destiny shut down her laptop. "I guess that's it for now, then. We can head out."

"Okay. Let me run to the bathroom. Be right back."

Destiny walked over to the mirror above the loveseat. She pulled the tie from her ponytail and shook out her hair. Deciding she still looked a little flat, she went over to her purse in search of lipstick.

Another call came into the office.

"I bet it's Margaret," she murmured. "Helped by an angel and on her way here. Good afternoon, First Lady's office. This is Destiny." Silence. "Hello?"

"Lady?"

"Janet?"

"Oh, praise the Lord! I didn't know if I'd be able to reach you, thought maybe if they heard it was me they wouldn't transfer the call."

"God worked it out for me to answer the phone. I'm glad to hear from you."

"I've wanted to talk to you ever since we came back there that Sunday. I didn't want to be there, Lady. Didn't want to be with Ronald at all. He found me. He had a tracking device on my cell phone. I'd brought it with me because if he'd seen it he would have been suspicious right away. It led him straight to my hotel door. I tried to be strong like you told me, Lady. But I'm not you. He kept pounding and threatening until I let him in."

Destiny was shocked but not surprised. A man like Ron was capable of anything.

"I'm so sorry for everything, Lady Destiny."

"It's okay, Janet."

"No, it isn't. I mean it is now, but it wasn't."

"What do you mean?" Silence. "Janet, are you there?"

"I left him, Lady, promised myself that I wouldn't let all you did for me be in vain. I'm scared out of my mind, but I'm away from that house. I don't know what I'm going to do. I left without much money. No car, few clothes. But I left him. With the strength of your words and the help of the Lord, I left him. And I'm not going back."

"Where are you, Janet?"

"North Las Vegas. A woman at the, um, post office found out about...my situation. She seen the bruises, and was supportive like you. Said if I ever wanted to leave home she had a place I could stay for a little while. Her, um, brother...travels a lot. I'm at his house now. But I can only stay until the weekend. He'll be back then."

"And you're sure Ronald doesn't know where you are?"

"No, ma'am. I left that phone right on the living room table so he'd be sure and see it when he got home and not try and find me. Didn't leave him a note or anything. But I'm scared, Lady Destiny. What do I do, now?"

"Look, text me the address where you are. Savannah

and I will come over. We'll put our heads together—"

"Oh no, Lady! I-I-I couldn't see Miss Savannah right now."

"Why not?" When Janet didn't answer, Destiny understood. "Ronald beat you again? Is that why you left?"

"I don't want anybody to see me like this. I don't want you to see me but…"

"It's okay. I'll come alone. I'm proud of you, Janet. Don't worry. Everything will be all right. God is on our side."

*

Across town, Ronald watched Janet's body begin to shake uncontrollably as he lowered his death-wielding hand from her face. He smiled, kissed her temple as he lowered the gun and issued a rare compliment. "Good job."

*

Savannah came rushing back in. "Whew! Okay, I'm ready. I…what's wrong?"

"Change of plans. I just got a phone call." Destiny looked up. "Janet."

Savannah dropped into an office chair. "You're kidding me."

"No. She left Ronald."

"No way."

Destiny nodded. "She's staying at a house over in North Vegas while the owner is on vacation. He's coming back this weekend. She needs somewhere to go."

"Where's her family? Her sister-in-law or some other woman who can help her?"

"She doesn't dare go anywhere Ronald might think to look. He beat her up again. She left with barely more than the clothes on her back, terrified and lonely. She needs some reassurance and a little cash." Destiny reached for her bag and placed her phone inside. "I'm going over there."

"I'm going with you."

"I thought of that. But Janet is so ashamed of looking the way she does. More black eyes and bruises, I'd imagine. I'll be fine."

"I don't like it, Destiny. You got involved in that situation once before and it backfired. Why would you put yourself out there again?"

"Because she's an abused woman, Savannah. Her spirit is broken." Destiny stood. "She texted the address. I'll forward it to you so you will know where I am. I will also stay in touch with you. Let you know when I arrive, when I'm leaving, so you won't worry. Okay?"

"Are you going to call your husband?"

"He's in LA remember? Taping a show for MLM."

MLM was a cable station geared toward inspirational programming that highlighted people of color. During his scandal their support never wavered and when his first book released they promoted it heavily, far beyond what purchased promo packages had required. The high visibility helped land his books on bestseller lists. When they called, he always answered.

Destiny looked at her watch. "In fact, he should be on a plane right now headed back here. If Nate knew about this you know he'd object to my going."

"He'd more than object, Destiny. He'd forbid it."

"All the more reason to keep this act of charity between us."

"Be careful, Lady."

"I will." The women hugged. "Promise, I won't be long."

Destiny stepped out of the side door and headed to her car. She immediately tripped.

"Oh!" She looked down and all around her and saw nothing that would have caused her to stumble.

That's weird.

She started her car, and placed the address Janet had texted into the GPS. There was a feeling of nervous anxiety as she drove out of the church parking lot. Heading toward the freeway onramp, the fluttering increased. An image of Ronald's face, twisted with anger, flashed in her mind.

Destiny swallowed the lump of fear that caught in her throat. "The Lord is my shepherd, I shall not want."

She continued to recite the 23rd Psalm. "I will fear no evil."

Destiny spoke the words clearly and with conviction. But all the way to North Las Vegas, an uneasiness remained.

26

The GPS informed Destiny that she'd reached her destination. She parked her car and looked around. It was a quiet, well-kept neighborhood of similar houses and neat lawns. The condominium complex was on the corner, an off-white building with a blue-trimmed windows and a slate-colored roof. There were eight units. Her eyes swept up and down the street, looking for any vehicles that looked familiar. Especially the black BMW sedan that Ronald Miller owned. She didn't see that one, nor the car that Janet usually drove. Nothing and no one on the street looked familiar. But her stomach still roiled.

Reaching into her purse, she pulled out her phone and called Savannah.

"It's me, checking in."

"Where are you? I didn't receive a text with the address."

"Oh, right. I forgot to send it. But I'm here. Everything looks fine. No sign of Ronald or anything out of place. It's a nice, neat neighborhood."

"Hey, Lady."

Destiny looked up. "Oh, there's Janet waving at me. I'll call you as soon as I'm heading back to the church.

Okay?"

"Desti—"

"Oh, shoot." Destiny hadn't meant to hang up on Savannah, but was distracted by watching Janet scan the streets. *She probably doesn't want anyone to see me. Not that anyone over here would know who I am.* Still, she understood the woman's paranoia and so hurried to gather her things and leave the car.

She crossed the street and stepped up on the porch that faced the block where she'd parked. Janet stood there, her eyes cast downward. The first thing she noticed was Janet's face. It wasn't bruised, blackened or bloodied the way she'd expected. Before she could process this, Janet pulled her in for a hug.

"Lady," she whispered hoarsely, "I'm so sorry."

"It's okay," Destiny said, confused at the sorrowful greeting and the fear in Janet's eyes. She was away from Ronald, had escaped his abuse. Shouldn't she be feeling better now? "Let's go inside."

She stepped through the door, then froze at the sound of a lock being engaged. In an instant, the atmosphere changed. The hair on the back of her neck stood up. She looked at Janet, who wouldn't meet her eyes and scurried away. Without turning back around, she instinctively knew that Ronald was behind her.

She looked anyway. There he was—tall, menacing, smirking. A predatory smile on his face as he came toward her.

She shoved past him, dashed to the door and reached for the lock. Mere seconds brought Ronald from the middle of the room to her side. He grabbed her around the waist and yanked her away from the door. Destiny had never been in a physical fight before in her life. Survival instincts kicked in. She fought to get free, scratching, clawing and reaching for his balls, wanting nothing more than to get a hand around them and crush away his strength. She twisted her body, kicked her legs, fingers reached behind seeking an eye to gouge. She felt skin. Clawed his face.

"Dammit!"

He clamped his arm tighter around her. She raised her leg and jabbed a spiked heel into his leg as hard as she could. He howled and fell back. Once more, she lunged for the door, threw back the lock, and scrambled to turn the knob. The door opened! She took a step forward, but her body moved backward. Destiny was snatched back into the room by her hair. Ronald slapped her with a force that spun her halfway around. Then backslapped her, cutting her lip with a pinky ring and propelling her body backward. A heel caught in the rug. The shoe stayed put, but she fell backward, banging her shin on the coffee table and landing against the couch where she lay sprawled, dizzy and terrified.

Two thoughts fought their way through the haze. One, *Janet betrayed me*. Two, *I didn't send the address*.

Shaking the hair away from her face and dabbing the back of her hand against the blood on her chin, she gritted her teeth against a tremendous pain in her side and sat up. A quick glance around the room confirmed the thought from seconds ago. Janet was gone. Had she left when Destiny tried to escape? She looked into Ron's eyes. A chill shot down her neck, clutched her heart on the way down her spine and puddled in her toes. The stumble, panic and urge to run when nothing had been chasing her all made sense now. It had been God's warning. She hadn't gotten the memo, and had voluntarily driven to the devil's lair, parked her car and walked inside.

The sound of a car starting broke the eerie silence in the room, save for both her and Ronald's heavy breathing. Seconds later she heard a car's revving engine and then tires meeting pavement as the car drove away.

Was that Janet? Has she gone to get help or taken the opportunity of his being distracted to save her own life?

Real fear jumped into Destiny's chest with such force that she almost hyperventilated. But she knew that to show panic or timidity would be her true downfall. She kept her head bowed until she'd regained a semblance of control, touched the back of her hand against the blood to stop its flow and wiped it on her skirt. Then she looked up and stared him dead in the eye.

"Is that why you brought me over here? To beat me like you do Janet?"

Having expected his blows to scare her into submission, Ronald was momentarily taken aback by her strength. He quickly recovered and pressed harder still, determined to break her, use her, ruin her.

"I've got much more than a beating planned for you, baby girl." He gave her an eerie once-over, fairly raping her with his eyes. "You were in my wife's ear for weeks, turning her against me, meddling in business where you don't belong. That wasn't enough so you falsely accused me of stealing and now my name and business are ruined. So yes, there will be consequences that include pain."

An involuntary shiver hit her body.

Ronald laughed. "Is that fear, my dear, or excitement?"

Jesus. Help me.

Forcing strength into legs that felt like putty and ignoring a face on fire and a throbbing ankle, both fighting for equal attention with the pain in her side, she kicked off the remaining shoe and stumbled to her feet. Ronald stood just a few feet away from her, hands clenched, breathing strained. What he probably mistook for a belligerent silence was actually an inability to open her mouth and form words. Still, no matter how it turned her stomach, she continued to meet his gaze.

Several tense seconds passed.

Finally, Ronald relaxed. "It's a shame to mar that pretty face. Don't make me do it again."

"What do you want?" In her mind, the question came out firm and steady but with a rapidly swelling lip and bitten tongue, she sounded more like a person half-drunk.

"Oh, come on now, First Lady," he said with a sneer. "Such a cold greeting for a faithful member of Divine Grace, until you and that pimp posing as a preacher trumped up lies to throw me out?"

"Is that what you've told yourself to feel better? That what's happened to you is someone else's fault?"

"My life was fine till you two got here."

"What do you want?" Destiny asked again, enunciating each word as much the swollen split lip allowed.

"Something I've been wanting ever since I laid eyes on you." He took a step forward.

Destiny took a step back.

"There's nowhere to run, pretty lady." Ronald came toward her, his steps slow and deliberate. It took everything within her but Destiny quelled her urge to recoil, and pushed down the bile rising in her throat. Still, she flinched when he raised his hand. He didn't slap her again. He entwined his fingers into her hair, twirling strands around his finger. "I'm going to have my way with you. Then I'm going to sell you back to your husband and use the money to start a new life." Destiny remained silent. "How much do you think he loves you? Do you think he has five hundred thousand dollars' worth of love? A million?"

"The church knows where I am. Savannah has this address. If she doesn't hear from me every fifteen minutes, she knows to call the police."

"Thank you for telling me that. I don't like surprises. So what you're going to do is call her right now and let her know that you're fine. That you and your dear Christian sister are going to...let's see...it's Wednesday, prayer night, so you and Janet are going to be in prayer and wish not to be disturbed."

Ronald looked around, saw Destiny's purse on the floor and grabbed it. A quick rummage through its contents produced her phone. "Call her."

"No."

Ronald calmly pulled out a gun and pointed it at her face. "You'll not only call her but if you want to stay alive, you'll do whatever else I ask."

27

Nate landed at the airport and headed for ground transportation. He'd texted Ben as soon as the plane landed and knew his friend would be waiting for him downstairs. As he navigated through slot machine rows and past boutiques and restaurants he tried to reach Destiny once again. It was the third try in two hours, so he didn't leave a message. He couldn't imagine a reason for her not returning his calls or sending a text at least. The lack of communication left him a little miffed but even more, worried. This wasn't like her at all.

"What's up, Preach!"

"You got it, man."

Nate and Ben shared a soul brother's handshake and began walking toward McCarran International Airport's short-term parking structure.

"How was your trip?"

"Good, actually. The interview went better than I thought."

"Did they tape it at the station?"

"No, we were over at Stan Lee's church. He's the president of the Total Truth organization. My interview segued into a piece about them."

They reached the car. Nate placed his carryon in the

trunk and slumped into the passenger seat.

Ben got in, started up the car, and looked over at his pastor as he eased out of the stall. "You all right?"

"A little tired. And a little upset."

"What's going on, man?"

"I can't reach Destiny." Nate pulled out his phone again. "She knows I worry when she disappears."

"Did you call Savannah, or the nanny?"

"I called home. Meagan said that Destiny has been gone since this morning. No answer when I called her cell phone or the church."

"Savannah didn't answer?" Nate shook his head. "They're probably off somewhere together. Getting their hair or nails done, something where they can't access their phones."

"You might be right."

"I'll try Savannah again though if you'd like."

"Yes, Ben, I would appreciate it. Thanks, man."

"No problem." Ben tapped the phone icon on the steering wheel. "I'll try her cell first since you say she didn't answer the church phone."

"Hey, honey!"

"Hey, baby. Where are you?"

"I'm at the mall. We finished a little early today so I thought I'd take advantage of doing a little shopping for the kids without them around."

"Oh, okay. Destiny's there, too?"

"No, she's not with me. She's visiting a church member."

"Who?" Nate asked.

A brief pause and then, "Pastor?"

"Yes, it's Nate. Who is Destiny visiting?" No answer. "Savannah? Did you hear me? Where is my wife?"

"She didn't want you to know, Nate, but she went to see Janet."

"She what?"

"It's not what you think," Savannah said in a rush. "She's not at their house. Janet finally left Ronald and is hiding out at a friend's house, someone Ronald doesn't know. She's safe there, but left home with barely more than the clothes on her back. Destiny went over to give her a little money and a lot of encouragement."

"How long ago was that?" Nate asked.

"About an hour, I'd say. I was worried too, Pastor, and made her promise to call me."

"Has she? Because I've been calling and not getting an answer."

"I talked to her about thirty minutes ago."

Nate heaved a relieved sigh. "Thank God."

Ben reached over and slapped Nate on the shoulder. "Told you she was all right, Doc."

"Was she heading back to the church?"

"She and Janet were going to pray, grab some spicy chicken wings and then head to church."

Nate froze. "Spicy wings? That's what she told you?"

"Uh-huh. She and I were heading out to grab a bite right before Janet called, but she went directly there instead."

He slowly sat up, his hands cold and clammy. "And you're sure she said spicy chicken wings?"

"Positive, Pastor. It caught me off guard too because in all the times we've eaten out I couldn't remember her ever ordering any. But that's what she said, that she had a taste for hot, spicy chicken wings and Janet knew where they could get some. She said it more than once."

"Savannah, give me the address where Janet is staying."

"I don't have it."

Nate's panic rose notches. "Who does?"

"I...I don't know. Destiny was supposed to text me the address but obviously forgot. She called though, Pastor, once she arrived at the house. Said Janet was there and everything was fine."

Nate reached for his phone, clearly agitated.

Ben did a double take. "What's wrong, Nate?"

Ignoring Ben's question, Nate barked into the phone. "Deacon, I'm about ten minutes from the church and need to see Officer Wright as soon as I get there. Have him meet me in my office. Gather security, too. We've got a problem."

"What is it, Reverend?" Savannah's voice was filled with panic.

"I don't know but Destiny is definitely not okay. She was trying to send you some kind of message with that statement."

"What makes you think that?" Ben asked.

"She had an allergic reaction to them once and absolutely hates spicy chicken wings."

*

Melody stepped out of the marble shower, the rain forest showerhead totally revitalizing a body that Harrison had screwed for hours. She was convinced that he just did this to make sure she was too tired and sore to be with somebody else, as if anal and vaginal penetration were the only forms of sex. Men could be so stupid sometimes. Still, for all the praise it sometimes received Melody knew the truth. Viagra was the devil.

Letting her body air dry, she left the bedroom and crossed over to a guest room that served as her closet. She searched between carefully organized rows of designer clothing, looking for just the right piece to wear. Sexy but stylish, something that showed off her assets in their best light. That was always important. For a boss in the skin game even more so. Harrison had suggested she take the day off, stay home from the club, which probably meant he was going to "interview" a few women to serve as specialists, waiters and/or high pay side chicks. Fine with her. It just gave her more time to spend with Fiona, the video vixen-turned-businesswoman with an idea that could be trashy or genius, depending on how it was pulled off. She wanted to produce an adults-only, Vegas-styled theatrical show that pushed legal boundaries, where actors and patrons alike would all be nude. Fiona made sure that Melody understood her partnership offer was not only for the boardroom but the bedroom, too. Both offers were being considered.

She'd just decided on and slipped into a silk wrap dress when she heard her message indicator. Thinking it was Fiona returning her text, she rushed back into the master suite and snatched her phone off of the dresser. It wasn't Fiona, but Ronald. What did he want? Melody made a face as she tapped the screen.

I've got her.

"Got who?" she wondered aloud, before texting the question.

Destiny.

What the hell? It had been a week since Melody had revealed her Thicke connection to see Ronald's reaction. She'd been surprised and a little pleased. Ron's ire mirrored some of what she'd felt in past run-ins with Destiny and again the other day at the mall. That's why she'd found no harm in playing into Ron's fantasy. He had to know she was teasing, and that paying him was a joke.

She answered his text. **Quit playing.**

I'm not playing. Have my money ready by tonight.

His quick comeback gave Melody pause. Ronald had taken the joke too far. Time to shut it down. **Prove it.**

"Now, send a comeback to that!" Setting the phone down, she headed toward the dressing room. Before she reached the door another message came in. Sure it was Fiona this time, she picked up the phone.

"You again!" Slightly agitated, she tapped Ronald's message.

An image was attached. "Shit!"

Melody tapped the keyboard and dialed 9-1-1.

*

Janet sat in front of the North Las Vegas police station on Carey Avenue. She'd been there for the past half hour, summoning the courage to do the right thing. Go inside and expose her husband. After luring Destiny over, she'd left as Ronald had demanded and was supposed to go home to wait for his next instruction. But she didn't. Couldn't. Her conscious would not let her. The shame at what she'd done to someone who'd only tried to help her was slowly but surely overtaking the fear she had for the man who'd forced her to do the awful deed.

Tears clouded her vision and blurred the police cars parked in front of the station as she recalled the incidents of what, until mid-afternoon, had been a normal day.

*

"I need you to do something." Ronald barked the command as she stood in the kitchen making a sandwich.

"All right."

"Now."

The mustard-covered knife stilled as she looked up, noticed the tension in his body and fire in his eyes.

"I need you to go somewhere with me. Come on."

"Where are we—"

"Don't ask questions, woman! Shut up and do as I say."

He drove them down the freeway to an area of town she'd never visited, down several streets and into an alley behind a condominium where no one she knew lived. When he got out of his car she followed suit and walked down a sidewalk to the back door of a lower unit. Ronald hurried them through an unlocked patio door. They went inside with her steadily wondering what in the world her husband was up to now.

She wished she'd never found out.

The back door opened into the kitchen of an open-concept layout. Beyond the cheery red, white and black kitchen was a dining room, separated by a bar counter. Beyond that was the living room. The front door was to their left and faced the street they'd turned off of to enter the alley. She watched as Ronald took a small duffle bag he'd brought in with him into a bedroom. He pulled out a video camera and tripod which he quickly set up. He fiddled with it for a moment, then barked at her again.

"Get over there on the bed. I need to focus this thing."

"Ronald, what are you doing?"

"What did I tell you about questioning me? Get your ass over there."

She did. Once he was satisfied with whatever shot he'd planned, he passed by her and left the room.

"Come on."

Again, she obeyed. A bad feeling stirred in her gut.

When they reached the simple but comfortably furnished living room he turned and placed his hands on her shoulders. "Okay now, Janet. I need you to listen to me and hear me good. You can't fuck this up." He'd pulled out his phone. "I need you to get Destiny over here."

"The first lady? Why?"

"I just need you to do it. Don't worry about why."

"How am I supposed to do that?" The bad feeling spread through every bone in her body. A strange house? The video camera? And now this request to summon Destiny? Whatever her depraved husband had planned could not be good. "I can't."

"You can, and you will. Call and tell her that you left me with just the clothes on your back. You're scared, tired, hungry, you know, the kind of bullshit that a goody-goody who looks down her nose at people and tries to get a woman to leave her man would believe."

"No!"

He'd grabbed her arm so tightly her fingers tingled from the loss of blood. "Bitch, don't defy me."

"Ronald, please. I'll do anything but that. She's been nothing but good to me. Don't make me lie to her. Please."

He raised his hand. She'd flinched and closed her eyes, bracing for the blow. Instead of a fist, however, it was the feel of cold steel pressed against her cheek that got her attention.

"As God is my witness," Ronald growled, his voice low, breath hot on her ear. "If you don't do what I'm asking, I'll kill you. I'll go back to St. Louis and not rest until your mama's dead and those no-good cousins, too. Their deaths will be on you. So what will it be? The first lady or your family?" He'd pressed the nozzle into her flesh. "Who you save is up to you."

*

The memories turned Janet's self-pity into anger. "No more, Ronald Miller. No more!" She beat her hand against the steering wheel, screaming the words now that she couldn't say to his face. "You've beat me, shamed me, made me feel less than a dog! No. More!"

Screams became a hoarse whisper as anger morphed into sadness and remorse. "I convinced myself to believe that you loved me. But you never did. I don't think you know how. You never saw what love looked like, didn't have the type of parents that I did growing up, nobody to show you how. I thought my love could fill that void. But I can't help you, Ronald Miller. So I'm going to help myself…and the first lady. May God have mercy on your soul. What happens from now on…is up to Him."

Janet pulled a stack of napkins from the glove compartment. She wiped her eyes and blew her nose. Then she calmly left the car, crossed the street, and walked into the police station.

*

Destiny lay in the middle of a king-sized bed in the room where Ron had dragged her after she'd defied his orders and refused to walk to on her own. She listened as he cursed his body, angry that so far he'd not been able to penetrate her, livid that his penis had refused to perform. She hadn't been rescued, but by this small victory she felt God was hearing her prayers nonetheless.

That's not to say the day had been without humiliation. She lay naked, made to take off her clothes at gunpoint and pose at Ronald's command. He'd pulled out his cellphone and took pictures, instructed her to sit and stand in degrading positions. Snapped lascivious shots while calling her "first lady" and "preacher's wife." He'd forced her to take him in her mouth. She'd chomped down on that dick like a hungry man on a hot dog. Only a blow to the head from the butt of his gun had kept her from biting it clean off.

She'd blacked out, and even after regaining consciousness kept her eyes closed, hoping Ron would drop his guard. If she could make it to the door and lock it, the bedroom window might provide an escape.

He left her side and paced the hallway located just beyond the door. This was her chance. There would only be one. With slow, deep breaths she calmed herself and summoned courage from the depths of her soul.

Yea, though I walk through the valley of the shadow of death

I will fear no evil. For you are with me.

Your rod and staff comfort me…

Surely goodness and mercy will follow me all the days of my life.

I will dwell in the house of the Lord.

She was ready. A countdown from ten to one and then it was go time. *Three…two…* Ron came back.

Destiny's heart sank. When Ronald began fiddling with the camera she opened her eyes the slightest bit and saw a fate worse than death. An erection.

Surely goodness and mercy…

Ronald turned to her, smiling, and walked forward with penis in hand. She scooted back against the headboard, raised her knees to her chest and clasped her arms around her legs.

He climbed on the bed and toward her. Destiny rolled to her left and dashed toward the door. He caught her, forced her on the bed and trapped her with his body. She fought, clawed, scratched, scraped. He caught both of her hands, and while holding them in a death grip used his teeth to remove a pillowcase from the pillow. He tied her hands to the headboard. Clearly, there would be no deliverance. For the first time since the ordeal began, Destiny cried.

Ronald crawled on top of her again, pried her vise-like legs apart and... *bam, bam, bam!*

"Police! Open up!"

Destiny believed the voices were imagined. But no, there they were again.

"Ronald Miller we know you're in there." *Bam! Bam! Bam!* "Open the door and come out with your hands up."

Ron jumped up and ran from the room. Destiny collapsed against the headboard, filled with relief and gratitude. God hadn't come exactly when she wanted Him, but He'd showed up right on time.

28

At the law office of Dunwoody and Abrams, tension was thick. It was the second time they'd gathered there in as many weeks. Kelvin quietly paced the room. Derrick calmly watched his son's nervous antics from the other side of the room. Princess appeared to be checking emails on her cell phone when in reality her mind was on Kelvin and Kelly. She didn't see a thing. Tai flipped through a magazine that she too wasn't reading while King worked through sermon notes on his iPad. A prior obligation kept Vivian from offering physical support but a text to Tai let her know she was there in spirit and sending prayers. Everyone silently wondered the same thing. Would Fawn show up this time? And if she did, would Kelly be with her?

Tai looked at her watch. "It's fifteen after."

Seconds before, Princess had glanced at the clock on her phone. "I know."

Kelvin whirled from the window that offered a pristine view of California's San Fernando Valley. "Where in the hell is she?" he asked through clenched teeth.

"Easy, son," Derrick said. "She'll be here. Have faith."

"I had faith last time. How'd that work out?" Kelvin huffed and stuffed his hands in his pocket, his jaw clenched from the effort it took to bite back the curse words ready to spew from his mouth.

Princess could only imagine the turmoil he was going through. Fawn had assured them that Kelly was all right, and that there had been no further abuse. But Fawn was a consummate liar. Since missing the last appointment Kelvin had neither seen nor heard from her or his son. So she understood Kelvin's comment about faith and finding it hard to trust the unseen. Everyone would breathe easier when Fawn walked through the door, hopefully with Kelly in tow.

Ten more minutes passed. Attorney Abrams, who'd been quietly working at his desk, reached for his phone. "I think it's time to have my secretary give Fawn a call."

Just as he got ready to push the intercom button, his speaker squawked to life. "Mr. Abrams, Fawn has arrived. Should I direct her back to your office?"

"Am I on speaker?" Mr. Abrams asked.

"No, sir."

"Does she have the boy with her?"

"Yes."

"Okay, good. Send them back."

With that news, everyone exhaled. Princess stood and walked over to stand by Kelvin. King set down his iPad and Tai closed the magazine and returned it to the coffee table, on top of several others. Derrick said a silent prayer for a calm and quick meeting. Mr. Abrams rose from his desk and walked to the door, opening it just as Fawn approached.

"Ms. Bennett! Please, come in."

One thing for sure, Fawn knew how to make an entrance. Rather than a meeting in a lawyer's offic, she'd dressed to walk the runway or hit the club, depending on the time zone. Her leopard-print jumpsuit looked painted on, revealing a perfect hour-glass figure and a generous behind. Gold-colored sandals with five-inch heels matched her jewelry. Her face was beat. Her short hairdo slayed. The scent of something musky and fruity escorted her into the room. In contrast her son Kelly, wearing jeans and a Superman tee, appeared to be an afterthought.

"Daddy!" Kelly broke away from Fawn's grasp and ran to his dad.

"Hey, little man!" Kelvin picked up his son and held him close to his chest.

Kelly pulled back. "Daddy, are you crying?"

"A little bit."

"Why?"

"Because you're coming home with me. These are happy tears."

Fawn took a seat without speaking to anyone. "Don't break out the champagne just yet."

Kelvin looked at the attorney who held up a hand as if to say, "I've got this." He handed Fawn a two-page document. "Ms. Bennett, if you look that over I believe you'll find everything in order and as you've requested."

Fawn all but snatched the document out of the attorney's hand. She scanned it quickly, turning the page to see the dollar amount. Her eyes widened a bit. She looked at Kelvin. "I asked for a million. You gave me two. Why?"

"I want this to be over," he said with a shrug. "I want us to move on, learn to co-parent, and give Kelly a stable life."

"But I still get to see him, right?"

"Everything is as we discussed," Mr. Abrams

answered. "If you'll look at paragraph three on page one, you'll see that the visitation parameters and schedule have been clearly defined."

"What if I change my mind and want Kelly back, or what if my son starts to miss me and wants to come back?"

Kelly answered at least part of her question by boldly stating, "I want to live with Dad."

"When Kelly is fifteen he'll have the legal ability to choose his parental residence. Until then, you must abide by this order or return the full payment, less the standard monthly amount of five-thousand dollars that would have been received under the old agreement."

Fawn reached for the pen, hesitating as she looked at the people around her and finally at Kelly, still in his dad's arms. She quickly signed the paper and pushed it across the desk. "I'm still your mama, boy," she said, her voice catching in a rare show of emotion.

"That's right," Kelvin agreed, looking at Kelly. "She is always going to be your mama. You got that?"

Kelly nodded. "Yes."

Kelvin put him down. "Go on over and show your mama that you love her. I think she could use a hug."

*

Across town, two officers and a social worker were knocking on Fawn's front door. When they left, Gerald was in handcuffs and his sons were in the social worker's care. Kelvin had promised Fawn that he wouldn't tell the authorities. But he hadn't promised not to tell anyone. Abuse had to be reported. Fawn's cousin agreed and did the right thing. Kelly had been rescued. Hopefully the other two boys would get help, too.

*

Nate looked at his wife. "You ready?"

Destiny took as deep a breath as she could with tightly wrapped ribs. "Yes."

It had been four days since Destiny's timely rescue from Ronald's clutches. She'd just been released from the hospital and was finally back home. Nate exited the car and walked around to open her door. She turned slightly to place a foot on the tiled garage floor and winced. "Careful, baby. How can I help you?"

"I can do it. Just give me a second." Nate watched Destiny carefully place both feet on the floor before reaching for the door handle.

"Baby, let me help you up." He placed his arms beneath her armpits and while careful not to touch her sore and bandaged midsection, lifted her to a standing position. Instead of removing them he slid his arms around her. "I'm so sorry, baby."

She hugged him back. "Stop blaming yourself, Nate. This wasn't your fault."

He stepped back to look in her eyes. "I'm your covering, baby. And I didn't protect you. I'm hoping you'll forgive me. Because nothing like this will ever happen again."

She kissed him lightly on the lips. "I love you. Let's go inside. I need to see my babies."

They were barely down the hall when the sound of tiny footsteps could be heard against the marble floors.

"Mommy!" Sade came running down the hall. Daniel was right behind her.

Nate blocked their advance, sweeping Sade in one arm and grabbing his son by the shoulder with the other. "Careful, children. Mommy hurt her stomach. So don't jump on her, okay?"

"Mommy has an ouchie!" Daniel's wide eyes took in Destiny's bruises.

Sade looked at Destiny with concern. "Who hurt you, Mommy?"

Destiny reached out and placed her arms around Sade's thin shoulders. "A bad man hit mommy."

"You had a fight?" Daniel asked in disbelief.

"I'm afraid so, honey."

"You said we weren't supposed to fight."

"Yes, I did. Especially sisters and brothers. But when a bad person attacks you it's okay to fight back."

"Did you beat him up?"

Destiny smiled and pulled on Sade's long, thick braid. "I did my best. But God sent angels to save me." She knelt down to Sade's eye level. "You're one of my angels. Seeing you makes me feel better already."

"What about me, Mommy?" Daniel said with a pout.

Destiny placed down her purse and got on both knees. "You too, my handsome Danny boy," she said, taking him into her arms for a gentle hug. "Have you been a good boy for Meagan?" He nodded. "That's my baby. I love you so much."

"Love you too, Mommy."

"All right, kids, that's enough." Nate reached down and helped Destiny to her feet. "Mommy's tired and needs to rest. You can spend more time later, okay?"

The kids gave Destiny another kiss before scurrying away with Meagan to get their promised treats. Destiny watched them silently, a smile on her face and gratitude in her heart. Had Nate not recognized her cry for help. Had the police not arrived when they did. Had Ron been able to…

She literally shook the thoughts out of her head.

None of what could have happened did happen. Best to keep her focus on that.

They reached the bedroom. Nate placed the tote filled with Destiny's things in the closet, then rushed back to help his wife sit on the loveseat.

"What can I get you, baby? What do you need?"

"A bath. I've been dreaming of an hour-long soak since the first time I felt Ronald's hand on my skin."

Nate clenched his jaw, the anger in him intense enough to cause a heart attack. "He's going to pay for what he did to you."

"He's already paying," Destiny replied. "He's in jail now and after being found guilty at trial, he'll go away to prison for a very long time."

Nate began to help Destiny undress. "Prison is too good for a man like that. Somebody who…" As he pulled off her blouse, words died on his lips. Silently, he unclasped her bra, removed her skirt and pulled off her panties. Her once flawless body was now scratched and heavily bruised. An angry red welt criss-crossed her shin. Carpet burns marred her back and legs. Tears formed in his eyes and fell down his face.

"It's okay, baby," Destiny whispered, taking his face in her hands. "These scars will heal, but I am still whole, remember? God fixed it so that he couldn't rape me. You're still my only man."

Nate nodded but couldn't speak. He sat on the loveseat, gently lifted Destiny into his arms and cried like a baby.

*

The following Wednesday Princess was in Las Vegas for the Sanctity of Sisterhood meeting that would begin the next day and end on Saturday. Kelvin had come with her and so had the kids. They wouldn't be staying the rest of the week, though. Just a couple of days of fun on the strip with their dad and then back to Arizona. They'd arrived that afternoon and settled into a comfortable suite at the Four Seasons. Now they were at the Thicke residence. The children were off playing while the four adults sat in the dining room, enjoying a catch up that was long overdue.

"I still can't believe it," Princess said, after hearing Destiny recall her nightmare in vivid detail. "I mean, what was he thinking?"

"That's just it," Nate answered. "He wasn't."

"He was like a man possessed," Destiny recalled. "Filled with evil, rage and hate. And the crazy part is that everything he blamed on Nate and me were things he'd either done or brought on himself."

"A narcissist," Kelvin said, reaching for his bottle of beer. "That's what you call somebody like that. Full of ego, selfish and only thinking of himself."

Princess shook her head, slowing chewing a bite of salad. "Pure insanity."

"No, what's insane," Nate began after finishing a bite of perfectly done grilled steak, "is who came to the rescue. Some of the very people who've wronged her the most are the ones who helped save her life."

"Right!?!" Princess exclaimed. "Melody Anderson of all people. Who woulda thunk it? Definitely not me."

"You couldn't have been more surprised than I was," Destiny said. "When the investigator shared that information, that she'd called 9-1-1, I was dumbstruck. And when he added that Janet had reported it too, I was stick-a-fork-in-it done."

Nate frowned. "It's no more than what she should have done. She's the one who lured you over there."

"Because a gun was being held to her head. That

woman has been through way more trauma than I experienced. Over twenty years' worth. I don't know how she endured it without losing her mind."

"But God..." Princess said softly.

Destiny nodded. "Amen."

"Ben heard today that she's moving back to Missouri," Nate added, to Destiny's obvious surprise.

"To her family? That's wonderful."

Nate nodded. "I thought so, too. Hopefully she'll be able to get her life back."

"Our prayers have been answered," Destiny beamed.

Nate simply nodded and smiled.

Kelvin looked at Destiny. "Tell me again how Melody was involved."

"She knew Ron from the gentlemen's club she runs with her boyfriend. He was a regular. They became friends. She said he mentioned Divine Grace and had nothing good to say about about Nate and me. When he came in grumbling and threatening to harm us, Melody thought he was just blowing off steam. She played along to make him feel better, never dreaming he'd take things so far. Good thing she did, otherwise the police may not have found me."

"They would have found you," Nate countered. "Because Janet went down to the station. I'm not so convinced that Melody's role in this situation is as innocent and convenient as her story to the police would suggest. That girl's been nothing but trouble for us since we've known her. I don't trust her for a minute. For all we know, she might have been part of the scheme."

Destiny wiped her mouth with a napkin. "Whether or not that's true, I won't speculate. All I know is when it all came down, she did the right thing."

"And just in time because man, I had about twenty-five men ready to ride through the city—gang members, veterans, a couple off-duty police, all determined to find you."

Kelvin cracked up. "Man, a whole posse! You weren't playing!"

The look he gave Destiny made her melt. "Not at all. My baby was in trouble. And I would have done anything, and I do mean anything to save her life."

"In that case," Destiny replied, "I'm glad it was the police who first arrived on the scene."

"I'm glad of that, too," Nate responded. "Because I think the sentence for first-degree murder is life without parole."

Princess smirked. "And to think this was the man most thought no one woman could ever tame."

Nate's smile was part sly, part sheepish as he replied, "Get with the right woman, your soulmate and heartbeat, and even Satan could get saved."

Kelvin held up his glass. "Well I say cheers to having Destiny returned to us safely."

The others held up their glasses and toasted.

"Speaking of returns," Destiny segued, "how's life with Kelly and the family of four."

"Really good," Princess replied. She looked at Kelvin with love-filled eyes. "I don't know how I let resentment and unforgiveness set me at odds with my husband and block my love for that boy. Kelly's a great kid—smart, kind, obedient. Kiara is totally in love with her big brother. And he's so patient and protective of her."

"I think it's wonderful they'll grow up with each other," Destiny said. "How have things been with Fawn?"

"So far, so good," Kelvin said. "She's called a couple times and will be down to visit next week. I'm hoping this arrangement opens a new chapter in our lives so that we can co-parent and getting along."

"Things are going smoothly but let's not get too hopeful," Princess said. "We are talking about Fawn."

Destiny raised a brow. "I don't know about that. If Melody Anderson can do good by me then Fawn can change for the better, too."

"Sister to sister, huh, girl?"

Destiny smiled. "Sister to sister."

"Are you sure you still want to speak this Saturday? Considering what you went through? You're looking much better but you're still healing, both inside and out. Do you think standing before a crowd of women and delivering a speech is something you really want to do?"

"Lady Viv is concerned, too. But I refuse to let what happened change these plans. In fact, having gone through the worse time of my life and with God's help come out on the other side, makes me even more determined to be there on Saturday. That test, as horrifying as it was, has given me a testimony. Before, I wondered about what kind of message I had for these women. Now, I have something to say."

29

Vivian sat on the raised dais and observed the crowd that filled the Las Vegas Convention Center's largest meeting space. When she held the first Sanctity of Sisterhood meeting almost ten years ago, she never imagined it would become an annual conference and had no idea how big the now incorporated organization would grow. Yet today, every seat in the two-thousand-capacity auditorium was filled, with more attendees sitting in an overflow room where activities could be viewed on a large screen. In addition to the annual conference they held three regional meetings a year, and oversaw hundreds of SOS chapters from all over the country, London and several Caribbean cities as well. The saying that God's plan for us was often bigger than our own was definitely true. God had blessed this vision beyond what she could have imagined. Her heart overflowed with joy and wonder at God's goodness.

She watched her dear friend, former pastor's wife and talk show hostess-turned-motivational speaker, Carla Chapman, hold the audience in the palm of her hand. Her fiery oratory, down-to-earth demeanor and wicked sense of humor made her instantly relatable. Her plus-sized confidence inspired those whose extra pounds had led to low self-esteem. She was the perfect person to set the stage for what Vivian felt sure would be an uplifting, inspiring and emotional afternoon. Carla finished her rousing welcome and turned the service over to the praise and worship team. After an upbeat praise song, former praise dance instructor Hope Taylor took the stage, along with four other young ladies, all dressed in white. The first chords of *Let Go,* a popular, award-winning song by gospel artist Dwayne Wood, had barely begun before the crowd rose to their feet. Vivian's decision to keep Destiny offstage until just before time for her to speak had been the right one. Her abduction story had made national news. Vivian knew that if Destiny sat next to her on the dais, the audience's eyes would be on her. Instead, they were focused on Jesus, their hands and voices lifted in total praise, letting go. She closed her eyes, remembering the recent trial that God had brought her family through.

Thank you, Jesus, for our little Kelly. For shining a light in darkness so that he could be safe, nurtured and loved. Give Kelvin and Princess the tools they'll need and the counselors their son will need. Bless his mother, Lord. Heal her broken heart, and teach her Your way. Heal the young men who abused him, and the person from whom they learned this abuse. It's a sickness happening in families all over this country. Heal and deliver, Lord. All of us need You. Don't forget me. Amen.

The song ended with Vivian on her feet, surrounded by other first ladies. *Let go. Let God.* Tears stained her cheeks, and many others. God was good. All the time. He never left His children alone. Even right now, His sweet presence filled the room. The musicians, in tune with the presence of Spirit, continued to play softly. *Let go. Let God.* She brought a lace-trimmed white handkerchief to her face and dabbed her eyes. Walking to the center of the stage, she hugged the praise and worship leaders one by one, then took the microphone from the lead worshipper, turned to the crowd and spoke.

"That's right, my dear sisters. Let go. And let God! Whatever it is, He can handle it. In fact, it's already done. So, right now He doesn't need your prayer. He needs your praise!"

The music built to a crescendo as a cacophony of praise erupted throughout the room. Women cried and shouted and danced in the aisle. For several minutes, Vivian stepped aside so the anointing could flow—could break every chain, destroy every yoke. Finally, with a subtle signal, the praise worshipper who'd led the song returned for one final chorus, which was followed by wild applause.

"Wow!" Vivian looked over to her sister pastors and pastor's wives with a huge smile. "I think this is what victory sounds like! This is what 'I've been delivered' sounds like! This is what 'I've been healed' sounds like! This is what 'I'm too blessed to be stressed' sounds like! Hallelujah!" She did a little two step and crossed the stage. "I'd better leave that alone. I'm not the guest speaker but I preach this thing because He's worthy!"

Shouts of agreement rained down as some stood while others who'd been standing sat down.

"Let's move on because I'm so full I could be here all day." She gazed at the crowd, her heart bursting with love and thanksgiving. "I, for one, have had an awesome time this weekend. You all came here to be blessed but let me tell you. You all have blessed us." She waved her hand toward the first ladies. "And we thank you."

The first ladies stood and applauded the crowd.

"Now it's time for our guest speaker, who will close the conference. When the initial speaker had to back out due to a personal emergency the Holy Spirit immediately whispered the name of who'd replace her in my ear. The name I heard surprised me. I'd never heard Destiny speak and, quite frankly, didn't know if she'd be interested. Well, let me tell you. She wasn't interested. Not. At. All." She joined the audience in laughter. "'I'm just twenty-four years old,' she told me. 'What do I have to share that will bless those women the way you, and Sister Carla, and Sister Tai, have done?' I didn't know the answer to that. But we both felt that God knew and stepping out on faith, decided to announce her as the featured speaker.

"If you didn't know about Mrs. Destiny Noble Thicke before a couple weeks ago, undoubtedly by now you've heard her name. The abduction and subsequent rescue got leaked and because of her husband's notoriety, was all over the news. We weren't sure she would be able to fulfill this obligation. In fact, I told her it was totally understandable if she did not. But she was adamant that she could and would be here, and ready to speak. So, rather than read this nice and neat little bio I put together a month ago I'm feeling led to just bring her on out here and let her tell her own story. Ladies, stand on your feet, and show your love for our dear first lady…Mrs. Destiny Noble-Thicke!"

A side door opened. Destiny entered the auditorium back straight, head high. She wore a simple white maxi dress that on her tall, toned body looked extravagant and elegant. Her naturally long, slightly curly hair was swept up in a ponytail. Her face was devoid of makeup—the row of stitches on her cheek clearly visible, bruises on her face, neck and arms dark and prominent. But from her shined an inner light that radiated a beauty no makeup could match and no bruise could mar.

*

Destiny was assisted up the stairs and after a nod to her mother and Kat, walked into Vivian's waiting arms.

"You've got this, Destiny," Vivian whispered. "Just open your mouth and let God use you."

Destiny watched Vivian walk back to her seat and then turned to address the crowd. "Isn't she amazing?" The crowd applauded. "Lady Vivian and the principles that lay the foundation for the SOS conference, this Sanctity of Sisterhood, have helped to shape the woman who stands before you today."

More applause and verbal agreement as the women applauded Vivian. Destiny took the moment to scan the audience. Varying expressions occupied the faces of those who looked back at her. Most were friendly, compassionate and encouraging, but Ms. Judgment and Sister Skeptical were definitely in the building. Mr. Envy and Brother I-Can't-Stand-You were present, too. It was all good. This wasn't a popularity contest. She didn't need everyone present to like her. But she hoped they all would listen.

"Good afternoon, everyone. Recently, I learned how quickly life can be changed, threatened, even taken away. So when I tell you it's a blessing to be here? I mean it.

"Lady Viv is right. When she called about needing a speaker for this conference, I thought she had the wrong number. But she believed in me and even more, God did. I came up with a title, *Sister to Sister*, inspired by the words contained in our pledge. A few weeks ago, I sent her the outline. She said the concept was good but that I needed to make it personal, something I knew would be hard to do. I'm a private person who likes to mind her own business. And then life happened and my business got reported on the ten o'clock news." She paused as tears threatened, swallowed them, and went on. "God spared my life and I lost all fear about exposing who I am because doing so may help somebody. So today I'm here to talk sister to sister, for real.

"My name is Destiny Noble Thicke. I'm from a small town in central Texas. When I was little I asked my mom why she named me Destiny. She told me it was because I was born for a reason. That I had a purpose."

Destiny looked at Simone, and smiled. Simone nodded and gave a slight wave to those now looking her way.

Destiny continued. "She said she knew this from the moment, the second, I entered the world. Of course as a little girl, I didn't understand any of what she was saying. That all changed when at the age of twelve I fell in love with the man who is now my husband, the father of my children and the love of my life, Reverend Nathaniel Thicke. I knew that whatever my destiny was it would happen with him.

"I know what you're thinking. It's written all over some of your faces. What does a twelve-year-old know about love?" She shrugged. "Nothing. I knew absolutely nothing about love and little about God and how He speaks to us, if at all. But I had an unwavering knowing in every fiber of my being that that man was my husband. When I was sixteen years old God told Nathan what He'd told me.

"Well, as you can imagine, the ish hit the fan." She waited as the audience laughed. "My mother, Kat, everyone was upset. Kat is what I call my grandmother y'all because," Destiny whispered dramatically into the microphone, "she's allergic to the G-word. Grandmother."

Kat scowled and shook a playful finger at Destiny. Amid audience chuckles her eyes gleamed with pride.

"Their displeasure was understandable. Not then. Then the only thing I understood was wanting to be with Nate. But I understand now. I was sixteen. He was twenty-eight, twelve years my senior. Much too old for me. They thought I was way too young for any relationship, much less one as serious as that which Nate intended. From the start he made his intent to marry me very clear. My family wasn't trying to hear that. They wanted me to go to college and have careers. Which I did, by the way. Graduated from Southern in three years so I could get back to my man!

"The women who raised me thought that Nate just wanted to take advantage of my youth and inexperience. Any of y'all who've seen my husband knows that's exactly what I wanted him to do!"

Some frowns deepened, but others opened up to a story that as it had unfolded in real time had occupied the church gossip lines for months.

"It was his mother, whom I lovingly call Ma'Net, who brought a different perspective to the conversation." Destiny found her sitting between Simone and a church matron named Mama Max, and blew her a kiss. "God had spoken to her, too.

"Fast forward a couple years, and I'm a wife and a baby mama." This description brought the intended chuckles. "Some hard knocks and let downs but overall as happy as can be. Have any of you heard the phrase 'be careful what you pray for because you might get it'?" The crowd murmured in agreement.

"Yes, Lord!" Carla bellowed. "Got it, too!" She finished shaking her head.

Destiny turned to her. "I'm sure there were times you questioned that desire," Destiny said, before returning her attention to the audience now at rapt attention. "What happened next caused me to question everything I thought God told me. Nate was caught on tape and he wasn't preaching the gospel. He was having sex."

A few gasps from those who'd been on the moon when this national-breaking story made the news.

Destiny addressed them. "Oh, you think that's bad? There's more. The woman on the tape was my then best friend." More sounds of disbelief. "Yes, a friend who knew all about me and Nate. And still, even that is not the worst of it. No, the worst happened when the videotape got spliced into a gospel cruise promotion that aired at a national convention attended by thousands. That's when the drama really started! As many if not most of you know, Nate lost his ministry. The backlash, gossip and outcry was so great that we fled the country in shame, sought refuge in Turks and Caicos. Side note? If you're looking for a place to hide, there are worse choices than the Caribbean."

She smiled at the attendees. Though still present, the number of frowns continued to diminish. Bright eyes and wide smiles showed that most were clearly enjoying this woman's courage to be "naked and not afraid," to strip down and tell her truth.

"When we got to the island, both Nate and I were at the lowest points of our lives. Nate had been preaching his whole life, as he'd been groomed to do since childhood. In his family, preachers went back for generations. His father and grandfather had journeyed before him and his great-grandfather had founded the church. So imagine being the stain on your family's legacy and the reason why the ministry's lineage at that church came to an end. He was devastated. And even though the tape was made before Nate and I married, it still felt like I was with an adulterer. The woman in the tape wasn't the only one he'd slept with while we dated. But that's a whole other story, one that I'm going to let stay in the past.

"I was hurt, lonely, confused, and sure that God had forsaken me. How could he have allowed this to happen? Where was he when the trouble was about to go down? He's All-Seeing, All-Knowing, All-Powerful, right? So why didn't he stop it?" Destiny paused and bit her lip against the tears that threatened once again. Support from the listeners filled the silence.

"Take your time, baby!"

"It's all right, sister."

"Help her, Lord!"

"We'd lost everything—our home, our faith, the ministry. Nate and I had lost the intimacy that bound us, and that we both treasured. My family tried to shield me from the vitriol being said and printed. About how I was too young to have married him in the first place. That I and the whoring, promiscuous preacher had gotten exactly what we deserved."

She frowned and mimicked one of her detractors, "God don't like ugly, you know," before turning serious again.

"I was only eighteen or nineteen then and let me tell you. I felt that all of them were right. That when God spoke to me all those years ago I obviously hadn't heard correctly. I felt like an abandoned child, hopeless and vulnerable, stupid and worthless. I honestly didn't know if what happened was something I could survive. But I had some women who were praying for me."

The tears began to flow and this time Destiny did nothing to stop them.

"Lady Vivian prayed for me. Sister Carla prayed for me. They know how controversy feels!"

Lady Carla stood, thrusting her hand into the air. "Yes!"

She looked at her family and friends seated in the first row. "My mother prayed. Kat prayed. Mama Max prayed. Ma'Net stayed on her knees. Not just for her son...but for me! They could have gossiped. They could have judged. They could have cast stones. But when my name came across their lips...they were praying. And I can tell you this for sure. God answers prayer!"

The first ladies stood and applauded. Many of the attendees followed suit. The organist added a riff of agreement as the guitar, bass and drums added a subtle amen. The impromptu praise break gave Destiny the chance to rein in her emotions. When she spoke again, her voice was firm and clear.

"Nate's spiritual brothers had been praying, too, and slowly the storm of our lives began to recede. We met some true men and women of God and began fellowshipping with a local congregation. I think it was three or four months into our time in the Turks that the pastor taught a message on the power of surrender. That night, Nate and I prayed together for the first time in weeks, maybe months. We released everything that had happened, surrendered it all to God. A few months later, Nate came to me with God's response. He told him that since we'd been willing to give up everything we were getting ready to have it all. That very night, Nate started what he thought was going to be a sermon. It became his first national bestseller. Give up everything," many in the crowd joined in as she finished, "and have it all."

Destiny was silent a moment, inwardly organizing a speech that came not from notes, but from her heart. "I'd always been mature for my age but in the four years we were on the island I grew up even more quickly. Nate and I spent a lot of alone time together, getting to know each other in a way that our prior busy schedules had not allowed. Our faith grew deeper. My relationship with God became way more personal than it was before. I didn't know it then, but God was preparing me to be a true first lady, and at the age of twenty-four counsel women who are much older. Even more, God was strengthening my faith, my belief and trust in Him.

"Had I not gone through the hurricane of controversy and scandal five years ago, I could not have withstood the tsunami that two weeks ago swept my life. I was abducted, assaulted and withstood an attempted rape. But as God would have it the woman I told you about earlier? The one who betrayed my friendship and confidence and slept with my man? Turns out she knew my attacker, had an idea where he may have taken me and contacted the police. Officers arrived on that doorstep without a moment to spare. God used the very one who'd helped ruin my life to help save my life. What the devil meant for evil God used for good. From that crazy coincidence, I learned three very important things. One, forgive everybody. Two, never try to figure out God. You can't. Three, no matter what it looks like God's plan is perfect. Always.

"My mom wrote a song titled *A Date With Destiny.*

It's really good, and not just because my name is in it," she added, with a laugh. "I was hoping it would be finished for today's service but, anyway, there's a line that says, 'got no time for drama, don't take it personally. I have a date with destiny.' See, my attacker was so angry he wanted to kill me. He thought I had a date with death. But God said, 'not so.' God said I had a date with the Sanctity of Sisterhood and this national conference. God said I had a date with my husband and my children, to help his ministry and to see them grow! God said I had a date with destiny, to share this testimony with you.

"There may be someone here who's insecure, has few friends or wonders about their path in life. Not too long ago that was me. But I stand here now to tell you, Trust God. He has a plan. You may have been hurt by a best friend, betrayed in the worse possible way. I've been there. Forgive them and move on. It makes life easier. There may be something in your past that you're not proud of, something shameful, criminal, violent, whatever. Maybe it was drugs or promiscuous sex, even prostitution. Maybe you cheated on someone, or lied or stole. You are not alone. What you did is not who you are. If you fall, forgive yourself. Get up and keep it moving. Because right around the corner your blessing awaits. And lastly if God gives you a vision, don't let anyone talk you blind. Don't let anyone talk you out of what you know you heard. He didn't give them the vision. He gave it to you! If God said it, no matter how crazy it looks or sounds, believe it. Go after it. Do you understand?"

The women, most on their feet, responded. Some nodded, others clapped, while even more gave verbal affirmation.

"At first I was scared. But now I'm grateful for this chance to talk with you, sister to sister. The devil tried to stop this, and put up quite a fight. But God forever has my back. And yours. It wasn't easy, but I made it. Or another way to say it, paraphrasing a quote from one of my mother-in-law's favorite movies—I may be black. And these bruises are ugly. But I'm here. To God be the glory! We. Are. Here. Thank you."

30

Vivian was the first one to her feet, followed by everyone in the building. She hurried over to Destiny and hugged her tightly. They enjoyed a brief, private exchange before Destiny walked over to where the other first ladies stood, embracing them all before taking the seat Vivian had occupied.

"Wow!" Vivian exclaimed, beaming at Destiny and smiling at the crowd. "Wow, wow, wow!" She joined the audience in their applause. "Was this the woman who thought she was too young to speak at our conference and had nothing to say?" She waited as the audience laughed, and those standing once again took their seats. "I guess I'm not surprised, though. If God can use a donkey to send a message, then surely he can use you or me.

"Destiny, dear first lady, thank you. That was...outstanding. I don't know if I could have done what you did just now, sharing so much of your personal trials and tragedies, especially in the face of these most recent events. But I'll tell you what. Nate had better watch out. Because a Hebrew-Greek bible and a few seminary courses and you can give that preaching machine a run for his money!"

Destiny smiled and shook her head. While sharing her

story had been liberating, she knew her lane and planned to stay in it.

"You definitely surprised me, girl. I think all of us in here are amazed. But guess what. I've got a surprise for you."

Destiny's brow furrowed.

"Shortly after the incident, I called your mother to offer whatever assistance I could provide and let her know I was not only praying for you but for the entire family. During that call she told me about that song she wrote."

The revelation was unexpected. Destiny looked from Vivian to her mother and back.

"She told me about it and she let me hear it. I was so impressed with what I heard that I offered the services of our stellar music ministry filled with award-winning, world traveling musicians. They've been working on the track and Destiny, the song is ready."

Destiny's eyes widened in shock. She wagged a playful finger at her mother and snubbed her nose at Kat. Simone smiled and shrugged as if saying, "guilty as charged."

"The finished track is only part of the surprise. The other part is the amazing singer I was able to get here and sing the song. Oh, you're right to look curious, Lady Destiny because I had to pull out all the stops and call in all my favors to get this much sought after superstar to join us today. But he's here.

"Ladies, helping us debut A Date With Destiny, a song that is sure to be a hit, is a face I'm sure you'll recognize. Please help me give a sanctified salute and a warm welcome to the love of Destiny's life, Reverend Nathaniel 'Nate' Thicke!"

Nate stepping from behind the backdrop took Destiny's breath away. Dressed in a tailored black suit, stark white shirt and black, white and gray tie, he looked finer than ever. Their eyes met. In this moment, if love were water, they both would have drowned.

As the band played the intro, Nate walked over to Destiny. She stood. They hugged. The crowd clapped and cheered. Most of them, anyway. But those who didn't were barely noticed. There was too much love in the room for hate to shine.

He released her, kissed her now wet cheek. Exactly on cue, he turned to the audience and began to sing.

"Life isn't always easy, but I've tried.
I've been through the fire, and cried.
Lord can you hear me? Where are you?
You said you'd always see me through.
And then came the answer. In time,
Everything He promised would be mine.
That if I believed I'd receive.
And on that is a guarantee.

Because…I have a date with destiny.
I'm going to get all God has for me.
I've got no time for drama,
please don't take it personally.
I have a date with destiny.

Some of you are listening and nodding your head.
Because you can relate to everything being said.
You feel like your whole world is under attack
For every step forward there are ten steps back.
But God sent me to tell you. Hang on.
The darkest part of night is just before dawn.
So if you're facing hell, all is well.
You are so close to victory.

You have a date with destiny.
You're going to get it all just wait and see.
Don't give in to the drama.
No, don't take it personally.
You have a date with destiny,
I have a date with destiny,
We have a date with destiny!"

Long before Nate ended the song the crowd was on their feet, praising God for whatever hell they'd endured and lived to shout about it. They'd heard the words and chose to believe that their lives had meaning, that their steps were ordered, and that their date with destiny was assured.

Only Destiny remained seated, mesmerized by the love she and Nate shared and the awesomeness of God. As the last strands of the piano chords began to fade, she became aware of Nate's eyes on her.

"I love you, Destiny," he said simply, once he'd ended the song.

She stood and glided toward him. He met her mid-stage. Again they hugged, but just briefly. Their bodies were on fire for each other and more than a few seconds of contact would have made this apparent to everyone.

She spoke into the microphone. "I love you, too."

"Sisters, this has been a pleasure. I'm actually on my way to church for a meeting, but I swung by here to do this for my wife." He looked at her. "I'd do anything for her."

Destiny blushed and looked away.

"God bless you ladies!" Nate gave Vivian a quick hug and rushed off to his engagement. The conference was over. Vivian gave closing remarks.

As she spoke, Destiny looked over and got her mother's attention. Simone stood and met her at the base of the stairs.

Destiny stepped down and hugged her tightly. "I see that first verse finally came to you."

Simone hugged her back just as fiercely. "Yes, baby. I was inspired again."

As Simone returned to her seat, an usher approached Destiny and gave her an envelope. She returned to her seat and discreetly opened it. Inside was a thank you card and a cashier's check. Her eyes widened as she unfolded it and saw the amount—$10,000. Shock and awe continued as she opened the card and read its contents.

Destiny,

I accepted your invite and came here and guess what? Lightning did not strike the building! LOL!

Destiny's head immediately shot up. Her eyes gleaned the audience but there was no way to see everyone in the packed room.

I left while you were speaking. Didn't need to hear the story. Lived it with you. But you were good. Sounded like a preacher's wife and everything.

I know we won't be friends again. That's cool. Different people, different worlds. But we've crossed each other's path for a reason. Maybe, as you say, it's destiny. :)

Inside is an offering for the church. I'm sorry. Again. Melody.

Destiny's smile was bittersweet as she placed the card and cashier's check back into the envelope. As badly as she'd handled some situations, somewhere deep beneath the worldly façade, Melody had a good heart. Destiny agreed that chances of a rekindled friendship was slim. But who knew? Life was long, complicated, and full of surprises. She'd leave it up to God and roll with His plan.

Tonight, there were far more important things on her mind. Nate's appearance had been a total surprise. What she had planned for tonight would surprise him, too. The children would spend the night bonding with their Nana, as Simone chose to be called, and Kat. She would meet Nate at the church around ten p.m. in a limo headed for the airport. Once there, they'd get whisked away by private jet to Nate's favorite San Francisco hotel. On the way there, Destiny would make a welcomed announcement. The ribs had healed enough for wifely duties to be resumed. Points would get added to their Mile High Club membership…in route to a date with destiny.

A Date With Destiny – The Song

Lead Vocals: JaJuan Turner
Background Vocals: JaJuan Turner, Dee Turner
Words: Lutishia Lovely
Music: Lutishia Lovely & Lois "LadyMac" McMorris
Producer: LDE Productions
Engineer: Dino Forino, Dreamteam Studios

Available on iTunes, Amazon and wherever digital
music is sold.

Discussion Questions

1. Early on, Destiny had suspicions regarding the state of a church member's marriage and vowed to learn more. Do you think she had a right to get involved? What would you have done?

2. While in love during this storyline, it's clear Nate and Destiny Thicke have endured their share of challenges. Do you think facing difficulties strengthen or weaken a marriage? Why or why not?

3. Do you think secrets in a marriage are ever justified? If so, give an example of when it might be better for "the right hand not to know what the left hand is doing."

4. Domestic violence is rampant in America and around the world. Statistics reveal that a woman is assaulted or beaten every nine seconds, and that one in three women and one in four men have experienced domestic abuse. What's your story?

5. Do you think the church could play a greater role in helping to end domestic violence, or is this a personal affair that should be resolved behind closed doors?

6. How do you feel about Princess's initial position regarding her stepson? Have you or someone you know been put in a similar position? How did you find a positive way to handle it?

7. Even though a first lady, Destiny made pleasing her man sexually a high priority. Their love life was adventurous and risqué. Should those in church leadership be held to a different standard when it comes to what is considered appropriate in the bedroom?

8. Melody Anderson was a determined young woman who when it came to achieving her goals felt the end justified the means. How do you feel about her position

and what she did to get what she wanted?

9. How much do you blame Melody for what played out at the end of the book? What about Janet? Savannah? Destiny?

10. It appeared that Destiny may have missed several warning signs about future events. What were they? Would you have recognized them? Share a time when you heeded a sign or listened to your intuition. What happened when you didn't?

11. The theme of sisterhood was woven throughout the book with "being our sister's keeper" part of the SOS pledge. Do you agree with this ideology? Why or why not?

12. The song Simone penned is an actual soundtrack! The author encourages you to download a copy to play during your book club discussion and then answer this: Do you know your destiny? Have you set a date to meet it?

Want more of the Hallelujah Series?
Take a peek at First Husband releasing in 2017!

First Husband

"Say it isn't so."

"If I did, I'd be lying."

It was two a.m. in Overland Park, Kansas. King Brook, the senior pastor of the Mount Zion Progressive Church, had an early morning meeting and should be asleep. But the topic of said meeting couldn't wait, which is why he'd risked waking up Derrick Montgomery, a fellow pastor and best friend, who lived in Los Angeles.

Derrick had indeed been asleep. Now he was wide awake and easing out of the bed so as not to wake his dozing wife.

Heading to his home office he asked, "What happened to our suggestion for a quiet, lowkey opening, giving the community time to adapt and, you know, get used to—"

"A church pastored by an openly gay couple? D, I tried to warn them. I said, 'look guys. This is Kansas, the buckle of the Bible belt. Don't draw attention to yourselves. Don't advertise, don't proselytize'. But real talk? To avoid any type of dissension or gossip, those doors would have had to stay closed and locked."

Derrick knew that what King said was true. For years, Lance Elliott and Malachi Clark had been prolific, sought-after ministers. They had also been in a long-term relationship. Many ministers in and around the Washington, DC and Virginia areas knew they were lovers. Some disapproved, a few vocally and often. Yet, their secret was closely guarded. Close female friends mistaken for romantic interests further aided the duplicity, and allowed both men to operate large, successful ministries. Then, eighteen months ago, Lance abruptly resigned as his church's senior pastor and relocated from DC to Kansas.

Six months later, Malachi gave his ministry in Richmond, VA a four-week notice and arrived in Olathe after spending three months in Africa, where his family believed he still lived.

The two got married in a quiet, civil ceremony, formed the non-profit religious organization Accepting All God's Children—AAGC—and began holding weekly bible studies at a Holiday Inn. Word quickly spread. Soon a Sunday service was added. Then another on Sunday night. The congregation doubled, then tripled, then forced relocation to a more conducive space. News of a "great church with gay pastors" continued to spread. Near the end of their one-year lease, the couple decided to find a permanent church home. Two months ago, work to turn a five-thousand square foot furniture store into a multi-faceted sanctuary had been completed. When King and others learned of its existence and inevitable opening, they knew controversy was guaranteed. The question wasn't if, but when, along with how large the brouhaha and inevitable media firestorm would be and how long it last.

"What's happened, exactly?"

King rubbed his eyes and stifled a yawn, his body reminding him that he was too old for ministerial mess. "I told you about the local reporter who'd been following them since shortly after they arrived and began meeting at a hotel."

"Right."

"She's doing a series on AAGC set to coincide with the inaugural services at their new church this Sunday. From what I understand the first article comes out on Thursday with a major spread in Sunday's paper. Once that happens, trust me, reaction will be swift.

"The religious right will have a field day, especially the ultra-conservative group Real Christians for Christ.

Their president lives in North Kansas City, thirty minutes from where their new church is located. They are going to stir up the pot, and with it public outcry from like-minded individuals and media attention from scandal-seeking reporters. Of course they'll be looking for varying arguments so if asked, we need to be prepared with a statement that is clear and concise."

By "we" King meant Total Truth, an umbrella organization for progressive ministries that recognized spiritual modalities outside of Baptist and Methodist traditions, including a relaxed position on gays in ministry. One high-profile situation they'd dealt with involved Derrick's church, the Kingdom Citizens Christian Center. When his wildly popular, multi-talented minister of music not only admitted his homosexuality but married his male lover, Derrick had faced a situation that had plagued Christian congregations for decades—how to allay the gay. Conventional wisdom dictated that the member be immediately relieved of his title and sat down until he repented and was delivered. Derrick had known Darius Crenshaw for years as a longtime, faithful participant at Kingdom Citizens, and a man who truly loved God. The organization suggested that Darius be removed from the high-profile leadership position and given a less visible role in the church band. Derrick followed his heart and made no changes. Though unpopular to most and heartily resisted by some, Total Truth abided by the decision. It was strongly recommended, however, that known homosexuals not be considered or selected for future highly-visible or leadership positions. The majority believed that to do so would send the wrong message. Derrick believed promoting unconditional love was exactly the right one to put out there.

"Have you talked to your father?"

King groaned at the question. "No, man, and I'm not looking forward to it, either. Daddy is straight old school, which is why he doesn't even know this ministry exists. I'm not looking forward to the reaction when he finds out."

"Knowing the Reverend Doctor, he'll be ready to march on the church."

"He's been on the front lines against homosexuality for as long as I can remember, almost voted Republican in the last election on that point alone. One quippy soundbite and Dad's voice could become the one for Christians who oppose gays in ministry or gays period. He probably wouldn't mind it, but that public spotlight could then very likely shine on the rest of his family. Namely me. And right now I'm dealing with enough."

That was true. King's three-year marriage to his second wife was on life support. Not that Derrick's life was without challenges. Recent observations had brought the very issue they now discussed uncomfortably close to home.

"I tried to reach Stan before calling you," King said. "He's out of the country but will be back on Friday, the day after this story breaks. Hopefully, we can have a teleconference Friday night to formulate Total Truth's official position on gays in church leadership and on this specific congregation."

Stanley Lee, who pastored a church in Los Angeles, was the current Total Truth president.

"Sounds like a plan, but that conference call is going to be explosive. Stan is your father's protégé and the Reverend Doctor is Stanley's spiritual dad. You remember how he felt about Darius. He's going to take a hard line against gays in general and this church in particular. It's going to take artful diplomacy to write a statement that satisfies all involved."

"Agreed, but we'll move forward in faith. I'll keep you posted."

"Thank, bro. Now, let's both get some rest. Something tells me we're definitely going to need it."

*

Fifteen minutes from King's townhome in Overland Park, Malachi and Lance sat in the backyard Jacuzzi of their über-modern suburban home, de-stressing from the day and discussing their latest interview with one of Kansas City's most preeminent reporters. Peyton Reid had taken a liking to the couple and a ministry she assured would one day be front-page news. True, perhaps, though not for the reasons she imagined.

Malachi stretched his six-foot-four-inch frame toward the center of the Jacuzzi and allowed his body to float. "What's happening is the exact opposite of why we moved here."

Lance sighed. "I know, babe. We neither wanted nor asked for this kind of publicity. But since news stories about our church were likely either way, I think engagement and cooperation were best. Hopefully that will lead to our ministry being portrayed in a truthful and positive way."

"You know this story is going to get picked up by the AP."

"Maybe not," Lance replied. His tone was light but his heart heavy at the mere mention of the Associated Press. "There are way more serious problems around the world than a Midwestern church run by two gay guys."

"I'm serious, Lee, and petrified."

Lance heard the sadness and angst in his husband's voice. He floated over and pulled Malachi into his arms.

"Maybe this had to happen, my love. Maybe a situation

outside of your control is the only way they'll ever find out."

"I'm not ready."

"You never will be." Lance floated over to a wide ledge on the tub, pulling Malachi with him. Placing his torso between his legs, Lance massaged his shoulders until the tension lessened.

"Aren't you tired of the charade, constantly spinning a web of lies to live a double life?"

"To keep the secret, I'd do twice as much." Malachi turned to face Lance with tears in his eyes. "He's always been so proud of me, calls my being his son his greatest blessing. Dad and I have been close all my life. I don't want to lose that."

"There is a way to possibly avoid it." Lance tenderly swiped a tear from Malachi's cheek.

"No there isn't," Malachi replied. "I don't want to lose you either."

"You're my everything. I love you more than life."

The tiniest of smiles crossed Malachi's face. "I love you, too."

Lance leaned over, kissed away the last of Malachi's tears. Their lips touched. The kisses deepened. They made slow, passionate love wrapped in the solitude of their hidden oasis. Afterwards, joy returned and laughter flowed.

Except a high-powered camera with a telephoto lens had invaded the private garden. And the person capturing every moment of their afternoon tryst wasn't cracking a smile.

Acknowledgments

Lovelies! Thanks for waiting! I'm happy dancing and filled with gratitude to present another installment of the Hallelujah Series, where this creative artist's book writing journey began. If this is your first Hallelujah read, don't worry. While you'll have to go back for juicy backstory tidbits, each novel in this series is written to stand alone. Brief summaries of the previous works have been included for your information.

With each book, there are always so many people to thank and usually someone that I forget. If that's you this time, please forgive me. The omission just means I have to write another book!

While preparing to write this note my mind went back in the day to the first novel, Sex In The Sanctuary, which was independently published by Novel Ideas, my humble d/b/a. Independent publishing was a different world back then. No digital publishing or eBooks, no online publishers to ease the way. It was strictly hustle and flow, baby, and I worked it like a Jamaican with ninety-nine jobs!

Back then it was dial-up and people like LaShaunda Hoffman, the creator of SORMAG, who provided a platform for authors like me, and workshops to help us navigate what was then foreign terrain. Later, it was PM Morris and Rachel Berry—may they rest in paradise—creating online meeting places where resources were combined and networking happened. It was thrilling and terrifying, but I was on my way! And now, so is LaShaunda! She has realized her dream of becoming a published author. I am so proud of you! It is a blessing to be able to publicly thank Parry EbonySatin Brown, the only published author who responded to my pleas for help as I navigated the uncharted waters of the publishing world. Reaching back and pulling up is the gift I now pass on to new, aspiring writers.

While processing a legal form for incorporation, the man assisting me asked about my company. I told him that I was an author and was writing a book. He asked the price. I told him fifteen dollars, but that it wasn't finished yet. He pulled out his wallet, handed me a twenty and told me to keep the change. He said, "That's okay. I'm proud of you for going after your dreams. Send it to me later." When later came, I called the number on the form attached to the receipt. Never reached anyone and couldn't make out the brother's signature to try searching the name online. Never saw him again. But his belief that I could and would finish *Sex In The Sanctuary* was a strong validation that I was in my lane and had the right of way! Eleven years later that framed twenty dollar bill is in my office as a reminder of my very first sell! Wherever you are my dear angel...thank you.

I am eternally grateful for requisitions editor Hillary Sares and Kensington Books Publishing. They were brave enough to take a chance and offer a deal for The Hallelujah Series, an untested meshing of genres that blatantly blends spirituality and sexuality, offering a no-holds-barred, unapologetic, nonjudgmental look at the church world as witnessed and experienced by this preacher's kid. Lovelies, as controversial and OMG jaw-dropping as some of my storylines have been, half the truth has not been told. Keep reading!

I am a proud member of the Kensington family and blessed to count my amazing editor, Selena James, among my dear friends. As we move forward into new and exciting territory, our publishing companies now join forces to continue the series that started it all. Hallelujah!

My agent, Natasha Kern, has been there from the beginning. Ten years later, that relationship, too, has gone from strictly professional (which it never was, really) to one of enduring friendship and spiritual sisterhood. Amazing!

As I joined the ranks of the traditionally published, so many others in this industry became a part of #TeamLutishia—supporting, encouraging, moving this little engine that could further down the literary track of success. Ella D. Curry, my promotions specialist; Debra Owsley, owner of Simply Said Accessories; LaSheera Lee and Read You Later, Ellen Sudderth and Nikkea Shareé are just a few of the thousands who embraced this series and helped spread the word. Priscilla Johnson, owner of PCJ Consultant Group, has always been a staunch supporter. She now uses her organizational expertise to oversee the Lovely Day street team, whom I call my avenue angels. They help promote the Lovely Day Experience from coast to coast. Thank you Lovelies!!!

A huge hug to Karla "KL" Brady, who is not only a wonderful writer but an awesome editor. Your insight and attention to detail are very much appreciated. Thank you for being an honorary member of #TeamLutishia.

Book clubs? Y'all are my heart!!! Whether two members or two-hundred and two, these word-spreading groups are the glue that holds the literary world together. I couldn't possibly name all of you who've read my books, invited me to your discussions, emailed me your (very strong) opinions (LOL) and story line suggestions and urged me to write the next one. Here is your date with destiny! Thanks for your continued interest and support.

To all readers who post reviews…THANK YOU. Reviews are very important. They can change an author's ranking, increase sales and ensure continued work from your favorite authors. You play a major role in our success. Your review postings are VERY MUCH appreciated.

To all reviewers, bloggers, radio show hosts, literary website owners, bookstores, newspaper columnists, TV personalities, celebrities, anyone using their media platform to promote all things Lovely, thank you. I am grateful for your help.

To my family, friends, spiritual brothers and sisters, EVERYONE who's helped this series stay around for nine books and counting…thank you. I may not have named you personally, but you know who you are, and you know how I feel. Much love!

As always, Spirit is my light, the Giver of this amazing creative gift. Every book I start or finish is proof of my eternal thanks and desire to live out the fullness of my destiny.

Praise for the Hallelujah Series!

"Once I started reading, I couldn't put it down. You won't either."
—Shades Of Romance Magazine on Sex In The Sanctuary

"A fantastic read that deals with celibacy, obsession, sisterhood and forgiveness."
—Books 2 Read Magazine on Sex In The Sanctuary

"A very good sequel to Sex in the Sanctuary. I enjoyed the way Lutishia kept the plot going...and the way the story flowed."—Urban-Reviews.com on Love Like Hallelujah

"Lovely does a wonderful job updating readers on the lives of their favorite pastors and their wives. (The book) will make you laugh and shout out loud."
—APOOO Book Club on Love Like Hallelujah

"Lovely boldly steps into the den with all that is taboo within churches. This is a remarkably crafted novel and a tremendous read."
—Romantic Times Book Review on A Preacher's Passion

"Lutishia Lovely has done it again...a must read."
—Urban-Reviews.com (Top Shelf, 5 out of 5 stars) on Heaven Right Here

"A stellar job. Well done."
—AAMBC (African-Americans On The Move Book Club) on Heaven Right Here

"Lovely once again expertly illuminates the wacky world of the devout and devoutly devilish."
—Publishers Weekly on Reverend Feelgood

"I enjoyed this book and recommend it for readers who want to read a book that will grab and hold their attention…"
— Rawsistaz Review on Reverend Feelgood

"This story will make you laugh, cry, and shout as you turn each page."
—5 Stars, APOOO Book Club on Heaven Forbid

"Lutishia is destined to become a favorite among phenomenal authors."
—Romantic Times Review on Heaven Forbid

"Hold on to your seat and get ready for the ride!"
—Carmen's Blog on Divine Intervention

"Balances the fine line between spirituality and realism."
—RT Book Reviews on The Eleventh Commandment

"Vibrant characters, artful storytelling, and an original voice make Lutishia Lovely worth every moment."
—Donna Hill, National Bestselling Author

Here's What People Are Saying About The Business Series!

✦

"Lovely creates a "lovely" lineup of characters intertwined into an interesting plot. A great story that deals with infidelity and the consequences. ...Fascinating new series."
—Sista Talk Book Club on All Up In My Business

"This book was heavily exhilarating. There were so many twists and turns that had me on the edge of my seat, flipping pages, just waiting to find out what would happen next. Every single character in this book was interesting, not just the twins. Everyone had a motive, everyone had a storyline, and that is what makes a book of this girth an enjoyable read. I eagerly anticipate the next installment to this series. Lutishia's transition from drama in the church to drama in life period was seamless!"
—Readers With Attitude Book Club on All Up In My Business

"All of the storylines in Lovely's latest are expertly woven together to create one big, dramatic tale. There are scenes in this novel that will make you laugh out loud and you'll barely be able to wait to find out what happens next. They are realistically written and the author does a great job explaining their traits."
—RT Book Reviews on Mind Your Own Business

"Lovely gives her readers a mouth-dropping OMG story. Just when I thought it was over, the story twisted and turned again to make my eyebrows rise. Fans of Lovely's Hallelujah series will soak up the second offering of this series with this new family. I cannot wait to see what will happen next.
—APOOO Book Club on Mind Your Own Business

"These books are so great and have so much drama, excitement and suspense, it should be a television mini-series. I practically took off work to read this book because I did not want any distractions. Lutishia Lovely is an author *where I don't have to even read the synopsis of the books. I know it will be a great story. Great Job!"*
—Behind The Lines Bookstore on Taking Care of Business

"Taking Care of Business was a great page-turning ending to the Business Trilogy. Cannot wait to read the next book by Lovely. I am a satisfied fan!"
—Amazon Customer's 5-Star Review on Taking Care of Business

"A great new taste in the literary world!"
—Carl Weber, New York Times Bestselling Author

The Shady Sisters Series Gets Mad Love!

"A delightfully wicked, suspenseful novel. I recommend this book."
—Book Referees on The Perfect Affair

"There is a plot twist that will possibly have you scratching your head and is totally unpredictable. This book will have readers flipping pages and talking to themselves trying to unravel the web that Lovely wove."
—AAMBC Book Reviews on The Perfect Affair

"A very fast-paced read. One could connect with the characters and the story flowed. Would recommend to others, and I look forward to the next book in the series."

—Maya's Books-n-Things on The Perfect Deception

"OMG!!! This book kept me guessing all the way through. I couldn't put it down. Very good. I can't wait until the final book. Can't imagine what it will be about."
—Amazon Customer's 5-Star Review on The Perfect Deception

"This reviewer was pleased with the nifty twists accumulating into a cliffhanging promise for the trilogy's final volume."
The Library Journal on The Perfect Deception.

"The story is both electrifying and terrifying. Lovely truly delivers in the conclusion to this trilogy. Read all three...they are awesome!"
—RT Book Reviews on The Perfect Revenge

"This book has more twists and turns than a roller coaster, a must read. This book will have you on the edge of your seat. Another great story!
—Barnes & Noble Customer's 5-Star Review on The Perfect Revenge

LUTISHIA LOVELY is a multi-gifted creative artist. She has written dozens of bestselling novels that one reader titled "OMG reads." Two installments from the Hallelujah Series were Romantic Times Book Review's Best Multi-Cultural Fiction finalists. *The Perfect Deception*, book two in the Shady Sisters Trilogy, was nominated for an African-American Literary Awards Show award in the mystery/suspense category. It was Lovely's first foray into this genre. Her current release, *A Date With Destiny* (Hallelujah Series) has an original title soundtrack written and produced by LDE Productions. Industry memberships include The Author's Guild, Romance Writers of America and the Black Screenwriter's Organization.

When not writing contemporary fiction, she lends her muse to the EMMA and African-American Literary Award-winning alter-ego, Zuri Day, and writes steamy romances. To some, this may sound incongruent with her work as a Reiki master, empathic and spiritual life coach. She will assure you that it is not. ☺ Lutishia gambles on life in the high-rolling suburbs of Las Vegas, where she enjoys vegan cooking, travel jaunts and writing nonstop! Her YouTube Channel is The Lovely Day Experience. Contact her at LutishiaLovely.com or on Facebook, Twitter, Instagram and Pinterest @ lutishialovely.

89735304R00164

Made in the USA
Columbia, SC
24 February 2018